NAARLEN

A NOVEL OF CHAOS AND FRUSTRATED LUST

PETER STAADECKER

All characters in this book, with the exception of Elvis Presley, Salman Rushdie, Frank Zappa and The Mothers of Invention, are fictitious. Any other resemblance to actual persons, living or dead, is coincidental.

The cover image "Arctic Geese" is a collage. The geese are © Robert Peter Staadecker. The background Arctic landscape is based on an image from pixabay.com and artist "OpenClipart-Vectors." The image was made available on Pixabay under a "free for commercial use" license.

The opening quote is used with kind permission of Clare Kines.

ISBN: 978-1-9990426-6-0
Paperback Edition 1.0, August 2021.

PRAISE FOR NAARLEN AND PETER STAADECKER

"So clever and funny. I love the story... The writing is totally superior and fluent. A delight ... really lovely and makes me snort and laugh out loud—which not many writers can do, but Staadecker does..."

"I laughed aloud, all the way through."

"How does Staadecker come up with these things? I loved his Bilbo Choir, this is as good, but TOTALLY different."

"Per Pederson is a human wrecking ball. But I love him."

"The reader watches [Per Pederson] step unwittingly into all kinds of disasters and remain blissfully unaware of the chaos he has caused. I want to shout out to him and [warn him]—kind of like in the pantomime shows where the kids shout out 'He's behind you' and the character can't get it."

"I can't figure out Per Pederson. He's mesmerizing, but complex. And what it is it with him and the Swedes? Can't they just get along? But then again, where would be the fun in that?"

"When I read '*All characters in this book, with the exception of Elvis Presley, Salman Rushdie, Frank Zappa and The Mothers of Invention, are fictitious,*' I knew this would be my kind of book. Twisted. Rude. Funny.
I was right."

***

*"The North has a long history of people coming here to hide.
It usually doesn't work well."*

- Clare Kines, retired Royal Canadian Mounted Police officer; Arctic Bay (Ikpiarjuk), Baffin Island, Nunavut. Latitude: 73° 02′ N

Contents

1. The Milk

Naarlanders. I shit on them.

In the six months of freezing Arctic darkness, they are depressed, gloomy and suicidal.

SAD, "seasonal affectiveness disorder," is caused by prolonged lack of sunlight. It twists the human brain, the endocrine system, blocks vitamin D production, warps human blood chemistry, warps the immune system, warps the human psyche.

Result: during winter, Naarlanders drink themselves deeper into suicidal depression and gloom.

Then comes summer with ISAD, "inverse seasonal affectiveness disorder." The twenty-four-hour daylight coupled with mosquitoes, deerfly, shadfly and blackfly ping-pongs Naarlanders between manic optimism and sleep-deprived psychotic irritability.

Result: In summer, Naarlanders drink themselves deeper into murderous irritability.

Naarlen. Latitude seventy-eight degrees north, way up above the Arctic Circle, an island and a city that exists only because of the mines: coal, palladium, nickel, and platinum. Six months of darkness followed by six months of light. Populated by runaways, drifters, fortune hunters, trappers, prospectors, dreamers and quick-buck artists.

Sometimes I think I'm the only sane one here.

Inge is my wife. A saint. An enchantress. A famous beauty. Flemming, from the National Academy of Northern Arts, has twice asked to do her portrait. So has Juneau, and he's a landscape artist. They see her beauty and her inner kindness. I love her as much as when we first met. More. But halfway through every summer the irritability gets to her.

There's a particular summer I recall. I saw the signs at breakfast.

"Morning, sweetheart," I said.

She made a face.

"Asshole. You forgot to buy milk, yesterday. Again."

The face was for the black coffee. The "asshole" was for me. Unusually strong language for Inge, but I've already explained what lack of sleep and twenty-four-hour sunlight does to Naarlanders.

I rose above this. I smiled amiably. When you live in Naarlen long enough, you learn how to cope with other people's ISAD. She was unmoved by my smile. The volume of her voice rose.

"I've HAD it with your forgetfulness. Be back before supper WITH milk or this time we're through for good."

She stormed out, slamming the door.

Witch! She knows how slamming doors gets to me when she's like this.

I stared at the door. Last year when she did this, I swore I would line the door frame with rubber to make slamming impossible. I hadn't found the time yet. The still un-rubbered door infuriated me. I threw a plate at it. The plate shattered.

"*Faen ta deg,*" I shouted at the door. "The devil take you," and I threw a cup for good measure.

Accusing me of forgetfulness was nonsense. I have a very good memory. I took out my notebook and wrote, "MILK!" in large letters. She is a wicked, twisted, gnome of a woman and doesn't deserve me. I thought of Juneau and his landscapes. Harsh, rocky, eroded canyons. That's what he paints. The earth's ugly bones stripped of superficial softness. In a flash, I understood why he wanted to paint her. How could I have missed it for so long? I had been blind.

No longer.

I would prove a point by buying the milk. Then *I* would leave *her*. *I'd* had it with *her*.

The cup I threw did not break. There was something cheering about this and my new resolve to have done with her. I filled the cup with black coffee, drank and smiled. Who needs milk to enjoy a Saturday morning?

Although it was Saturday, I dressed carefully, including jacket and tie. When you're this far north, it's too easy to let your standards drop.

The brown jacket had a tear that I'd been meaning to take over to Aarne for mending. I switched to the blue blazer, put the brown jacket under my arm and headed out on my errands. I forgot my notebook, but how hard is it to remember two errands? I said to myself three times, "Aarne and milk." The initials of the two words made a pleasing acronym: AM. I think therefore I AM. There's no way I would forget either task.

The sunlight was unwavering, but I felt good. I started our little ute, unplugged the block heater, and drove off.

Aarne is Naarlen's tailor and dry-cleaner. We've known and liked each other for years. A good man. Today he was fussing, almost frantic.

"I don't know what to do, Per. I need to mind the shop. Yulie's away down south, but Magnus is looking bad. I think it's that heart thing again."

I bent down to pat Magnus. He's a big dog, and was looking very sick. His nose was hot and dry. The edges of his upper lips were curled up, showing dry and white. His eyes were half glazed and bloodshot. There was no reaction when I patted him. His breath was wheezing in hot grunts.

"Aarne, listen, put Magnus in my car. Then you mind your shop and *I'll* drive him over to the vet."

"Oh, Per, you don't know how much that means..."

"Nei, nei, Aarne, it's nothing. We Naarlanders have to look out for each other, isolated up here at the top of the world, nei? And anyway, I like dogs. Really, it's nothing."

We loaded Magnus into the back seat, then I drove to the vet.

Konstanze is our vet in Naarlen. She's famously foul-mouthed, but a good vet. Everyone loves her.

"Morning, Per."

"Konnie."

"And that Aarne's Magnus?"

"Ja, ja."

"Put him on the table, please, Per."

"Oof, he's not light, ja."

"Hmm."

She looked him over while talking at me, then listened to his heart, felt his stomach, peered into his eyes.

"Did I ever tell you the one, Per... ?"

"Ja, ja, Konnie..."

"About the vet looking for her ballpoint in her pocket..."

"Many times, Konnie..."

"All she finds is her rectal thermometer ..."

"Including the last time, Konnie..."

"So, she looks at the thermometer in surprise and says..."

"Maybe the last two or three times also, Konnie..."

"Some bum's got my pen."

"O ja."

"Haa. Love that story. Fortunately, *I* have my thermometer. Per, hold his head, while I measure temperature down the other end."

I held Magnus's head. He looks at me gratefully. I leaned closer to whisper, "Good dog, Magnus."

Konnie inserted the rectal thermometer and he lunged at me.

I stared at my hand in shock. There was blood from a puncture mark, and he'd ripped my blue blazer.

"Son of a bitch!"

Konnie nodded, "I knew her. A German Shepherd."

She stared at her thermometer.

"Thirty-eight point five, all normal and look how he's perked up."

Magnus had jumped off the table and was growling at me.

"Probably just indigestion and overexcitement," said Konnie. "I'll write out a prescription. It will calm him."

She scrawled something on a scrap of paper and handed it to me.

"Tell Aarne to stop giving him table scraps."

"Bugger Aarne and Magnus both," I said.

Konnie looked shocked.

"Language, Per."

"He bit me."

"Did he, now?"

She bent down to pat the ugly brute.

"There, there, my sweets. Did the naughty man frighten you?"

The lying piece of jaws on legs swayed his whole rear end at her, in time with his wagging tail, trying to look harmless and seductive.

Then she turned to me in a less saccharine voice, "He'll be fine, Per, unless you've given him rabies."

"Keep the damn dog. You work it out with Aarne."

I walked out seething, and slammed her door behind me. That should have felt good, except the door had one of those spring-loaded mechanical arms that pulls the door closed at a geriatric speed. No matter how hard you tried, you couldn't slam it. What kind of anal-retentive nitpicker puts those on doors? Damn Konnie.

Typical Aarne to land me in this pickle. Typical Naarlander, self-centred degenerates the lot of them. I have no idea why I offered to help him. I don't even like dogs: mindless stomachs with teeth on one end and a sidewalk-soiling conveyor belt on the other. And sod Konnie. If we were down south, we'd have decent vets instead of this fucking foul-mouthed charlatan.

I walked over to the pharmacy to get some disinfectant for my hand. I opened my wallet to pay.

"I'll take that," said the pharmacist.

He reached into my wallet and grabbed Magnus's prescription. He read it, gazed at me in surprise. He started to say, "Very unusual outside of a .... outside of a..."

He swallowed the rest of the sentence, mumbled something, then bounded off with the paper in his hand. He was back in a trice with a bottle of pills, still gazing at me with wide eyes.

"These are GOOD. Very CALMING. Maximum two a day. You MUST take them with MEALS."

His demeanour had changed. For some reason he was now talking to me in a slow soothing voice. As though I might bite him. A day full of idiots.

"I'm not paying for that," I said.

He paled. His Adam's apple bobbed nervously.

"On the house," he said hastily.

I paid for just the disinfectant, walked outside and got into the ute. I noticed my brown jacket, that I meant to leave with Aarne for mending, was still on the back seat. It was now covered with Magnus's hair and slobber. I felt the rage against Magnus rising like high tide at the sewage treatment plant. I took two of the new calming pills.

I focused on what I had set out to do this morning.

"I think therefore I AM."

Aarne and Magnus. A and M. My chores were done. My mood lightened. I hummed to myself as I drove. On the corner of Second and Main, the lights were against me. There was a small van ahead of me, also waiting for the lights. Ahead of the van a very attractive mother—unusually well endowed—I mean, *really, really* well endowed—with an infant in a stroller moved through the crosswalk.

I gazed at her appreciatively. Suddenly I remembered.

"MILK."

The lights turned green and the van moved.

I have no idea how the van made me remember the milk, but thank goodness.

Was it, "I think therefore I AMM"?

Aarne, Magnus and MILK? But I also needed cash for the milk. My credit card had gone through the wash in my trousers. Then I ironed the trousers with the card inside. The thing no longer worked. Who knew credit cards are so sensitive?

I had to drop by the bank for cash. And that's when things started to go weird.

For some reason I was in an upbeat mood entering the bank. This is not usual. Banks and I don't have an easy relationship.

On Saturdays the Standard Naarlen and General Savings Co-op only has one teller on duty, Mrs. McKenzie, known to all as Grandma Mac. A sign of affection and respect. She's a delightful woman. A treasure.

I reached the front of the line. Just as I was about to make my withdrawal some yobbo tried to horn in ahead of me.

"Wait your turn, you mannerless cretin," I said mildly, and added "*Drittsekk,*" in case he needed to hear it in stereo.

I pushed him out of the way, hard.

Have you noticed how people get ruder by the day? Clearly, he hadn't read any etiquette books. He was back again. Trying to shoulder me out of the way once more. My mood of wellbeing was slowly evaporating. Not only was he rude, but he was one of those cross-dressers you hear about in the news from down south. He was wearing women's pantyhose over his face. Idiot. I was about to teach him etiquette and dress code when I noticed the ugly-looking revolver he was waving.

I bowed and said, "After you, Mr. Pantyhose."

He waved the pistol at Grandma Mac.

"Hand over the money."

He reached out with the non-pistol hand. Grandma stabbed it with a letter opener then slammed closed a three-inch-thick security glass partition. She mouthed something at him, which looked rude, and pressed a button on her desk. Sirens started wailing. I held my hands over my ears.

The cross-dressing robber did not look happy. Good for Grandma Mac. A woman after my own heart. A Naarlen treasure.

Two security guards appeared from wherever they were napping.

Mr. Pantyhose grabbed me with his free hand and shouted, "Stand clear or I shoot the hostage."

Rage filled me. That STUPID Grandma Mac. Why didn't she give him the damn money? Trust that senile old fart of a woman to screw this up. I would sue this sorry excuse for a bank into the ground, and her sorry ass too.

Mr. Pantyhose hustled me out of the bank shouting, "No one follows us or I blow the hostage away."

I tried telling him, "I don't want to be seen with someone who dresses like you," and, "Do you even know where those pantyhose have been?" but he barely heard me.

We hustled around the block to a waiting car. It wouldn't have been my choice of a getaway car. Too noticeable: Momo mag wheels, wide mouth double chrome exhaust tips, racing stripes, racing slicks on the back wheels, through-hood air scoop and tinted windows—almost black—all the way round. Mr. P shoved me into the back seat.

The man at the wheel said, "What?"

Mr. P said, "It's a holy fuckup. Meet our hostage. Let's go."

Mr. Driver screeched into the traffic. I could hear police sirens coming up behind us and hastily took two more dog pills. The fuckup gang screech into a right-hand turn towards our big bridge. I smiled to myself.

Once they were fully committed to that route, I said to the pantyhose man, "I have things to tell you both."

"What?" said Mr. P.

"Your mother dresses you funny, you have a run in your pantyhose, and your driver has shit for brains. The bridge is blocked for repair all this week. This road goes nowhere until the repairs finish. Peace."

I waved a two-finger peace sign. I don't know where the peace sign came from. Maybe the dog pills. I waved it again. At which point the driver screeched to a stop inches from the bollards blocking the bridge. Two police cars zoomed up. One blocked our way backwards, the second pulled up next to us, blocking the way sideward.

The policeman next to us was looking bored. He had three stripes plus a crown on his sleeve. A sergeant or some such. I marvelled at his calmness, probably not based on dog pills either. But then, Naarlen's police force is one of the world's best. They're famous for intelligence, bravery and determination. Yes siree, an honest citizen feels safe in their presence.

The sergeant wound down the window and peered at us. He couldn't see us through our tinted glass. He motioned us to wind down the windows.

Mr. P wound down the window just an inch, enough to be heard but not seen, and shouted, "back off or I'll shoot the hostage."

The sergeant shrugged, like a plumber talking to the owner of a flooded kitchen. Flooded kitchen? For the plumber it's not an emergency. It's a business opportunity. It's not *his* flooded kitchen.

The sergeant appeared to lose interest in the getaway car. His windows weren't tinted. We could see him clearly. He took a swig of coffee from a thermos flask, then said "Aah" loudly enough for us to hear.

Mr. P repeated his threat to shoot me. Then he shouted, "did you hear?"

The sergeant wiped the inside of his cup dry with a square of paper towel, and methodically screwed the cup back over the top of the thermos flask. Only then did he look at our car.

"Comrade bank robbers," he finally said.

His voice was very deep. A Russian accent. We get all nationalities in Naarlen. Like the French Foreign Legion, some people are drawn here by adventure, some are on the run from the police or alimony payments down south, some are looking for isolation pay, some have been barred from professional practice down south or defrocked, some cannot make it anywhere else. We hear all accents in Naarlen. Russian is common.

This Russian sounded like he could be Ivan Rebroff's twin brother—the singer whose voice spanned eight bass octaves. Ivan, not the twin brother.

I wondered if the sergeant sang.

I started to sing the chorus to the Volga boatmen. My voice never sounded better. Maybe the dog pills were good for something after all.

"Gospodin, bank robbers," said our sergeant, "nice singing. Is hostage bank customer?"

Mr. Pantyhose was confused by this approach. He prodded me with the revolver and hissed, "Are you a bank customer?"

I stopped my chorus long enough to say, "Obviously, dimwit."

Mr. P shouted to the policeman through the window crack, "Yes."

The sergeant nodded. "Is capitalist. Is bloodsucking oppressor of working class. Shoot him now, or I shoot him later, comrades. It makes no whatever."

Mr. P said, "What?"

I said, "What?"

I no longer felt like singing. The dog pills were not working so well. I took another two. Then I remembered that I'm supposed to take them with meals.

I said to Mr. P, "Do you have anything to eat?"

Mr. P didn't even hear me. He was focused on the policeman.

The sergeant looked sad. "Comrades, I applaud for you. You redistribute oppressors' wealth to people. How much you have?"

I was thinking, "That pathetic Naarlen police force. An international joke. Where did they find the last Russian Marxist? A museum in Siberia? In the third-level basement parking lot of some East German municipal building where the workers still haven't heard about the Berlin Wall? And trust that useless Naarlen police force to hire him."

Mr. P was more vocal. "What?"

The sergeant said again, "How much money you have from capitalist bank?"

Mr. P shouted, "Nothing. No money. We only have the hostage."

The policeman dug in his lunch box. He held up a sandwich and said, "Katia make this. Katia, my wife." He put it back into the lunch box. "No pickles. I hate when Katia forget pickles."

Mr. P shouted, "Can we go now?"

He hesitated, then added, "Err... Comrade Policeman."

"You have pickles?"

"No, Comrade Policeman."

The sergeant sighed. He shook his head slowly, still looking at the lunch box.

"You cannot go. Now you shoot capitalist hostage. After, I shoot you. Comrades, world is sad place. Never I ask much, but I must make living by shooting people. Russians are famous philosophers, no? We bear much. Always so. Is history of my country. I make peace in heart now for shooting people. For Katia, for me, for baby come soon, for pickles. Now, please, out of car. I shoot you through windows is bad. Bosses ask why break windows, why damage car? Capitalists always ask why you shoot car or building or factory or windows. Then extra paperwork for worker policeman. Two extra pages. Maybe four. Come comrades, worker solidarity. Step out of car."

Credit to Mr. Pantyhose for one original thought. He ripped the pantyhose off his face, put it over my head, unloaded the revolver, stuck the bullets into his pocket, handed me the gun and said, "hold this."

Then he shouted through the window, "I'm sending out the two hostages."

He and the driver climbed out. They ran to the policeman and thanked him for rescuing them. I was left in the car holding the gun. With a stupid pantyhose mask on my face. And I still didn't know where it had been.

I knew whose fault all this was. INGE. If she hadn't made a fuss about the milk, none of this would have happened. I was SO leaving her.

It would have been sorted out sooner if the dumbass Russian had listened to me. Instead, he put the cuffs on all three of us and we went to the police station to sort it out. All three of us wailing, "I'm the hostage" — "No, me" — "No, me. I'm the real hostage."

Correction. They wailed. I said it with quiet dignity.

The evidence was in my favour. The driver had his prints on the steering wheel and squealed on his buddy, the original Mr. Pantyhose. Mr. Pantyhose had the revolver bullets in his pocket with his fingerprints all over them. The bank surveillance videotape, plus that senile old fart Grandma Mac, confirmed I was the customer and Mr. Pantyhose was the robber.

The sergeant, though, was reluctant to let me loose. He sulked as only a Russian can sulk. I expected any minute he would take off a shoe and bang it on his desk. Thing is, when he put the cuffs on me, I called him a bourgeois lackey of the fascist state and a closet Trotskyite.

Who knew he was such a sensitive soul? Why do sensitive people gravitate to police work? If I wasn't going to leave her, I'd ask Inge. She's good with interpreting these emotional issues.

"How your hand get wound?" the Russian sergeant demanded.

He was still hoping I was the one that Grandma Mac stabbed with the letter opener. I told him about Konnie, the thermometer and Magnus. His eyes went piggly-narrow with suspicion. What did this champion of justice do? He called in the sex crimes unit and had them interrogate me about the relationships between Konnie, Magnus, and me.

Some people's minds naturally sink to the gutters. The man was pathetic.

I told him, "I hope your pickles develop boils and your boils develop pickles. Think of that next time Katia makes you a sandwich."

His face turned pale. But my comments earned me a nasty piece of revenge on the sergeant's part: he "forgot" to tell the sex crimes unit that Magnus is a dog and Konnie is a vet. I was slow to pick up on this confusion among my new interrogators, because I took two more dog pills and ignored most of their idiot questions. It prolonged my interview with them by an extra half hour. I didn't know what they were yabbering on about, but much later when I sat up, smacked my forehead and shouted "MILK," they muttered, "HA!" Then they wrote at least half a page of notes.

Milk. Damn. I still didn't have cash. If I was quick, I might just make it before the bank closed. I got up to leave. The sex crimes unit was still catching up their notes on the milk.

"We're not done, Mister Pederson."

"Then you stay until you finish," I told them.

In Naarlen, that's a subtle insult. We have all kinds of northerners in Naarlen. We have Faroese, Shetlanders, Hebrideans, Icelanders, Canucks, Inuit, Siberians, Greenlanders, Danes, Swedes, and Norwegians by the bucketload, but Finns and all things Finnish are viewed with suspicion. Don't ask me why.

I went to each one, pointing at each one in turn and repeating as I left, "You finish, you finish."

On my way out of the police station, I passed another sergeant. Three stripes but no crown. His radio was telling him to get his ass to the same bridge I had just left. They had a man threatening to jump off the bridge, name of Lundgren. The man, not the bridge.

"Lundgren?" I said to the new sergeant.

"You know him, Sir?"

"Oh, ja. Ja, sure. I know Lundgren."

"You come with me please, Sir."

The name plate on his chest read, "David Panigoniak." Judging by that, he was a native Naarlander. A compact, efficient looking man. He grabbed me and hustled me off to his patrol car, then back to the bridge. At least he was polite about it—called me "Sir," but his grip was iron. Velvet glove politeness over a steel core.

Lundgren was balancing on the parapet over the harbour. He was wearing very dark sunglasses, sandals and a raincoat, which was weird. Plus, he had a shopping bag in his right hand. The bag was one of those printed reusable shopping bags. It was marked with images of the Statue of Liberty and the words "Shop New York City."

I said to the sergeant, "What's the fuss? Teenagers do that jump all summer to show off. Now the ice is gone, it's just a jump into water."

The sergeant shook his head.

"It's high. What if he hurts himself?"

"Call the harbour police. Let them fish him out."

The sergeant froze in mid-stride.

"The harbour police? Good-for-nothing but sitting on their bums. Obstruction and paperwork at every turn. Take all the credit for successes and blame us regular police for any failures. I'll slit my own throat before I speak to them. And my aunt works for them too. We don't speak. She's worst of the lot."

He spat.

Typical Naarlen. No two city departments will ever co-operate. In Naarlen they say that if a child drops into a well, no one will save it.

The fire department will say, "It's a well, dumbo, the water won't burn, call the police."

The police will say, "Unless the kid's wanted for a crime, call the paramedics, a-hole."

The paramedics will say, "You don't know where the parents are? Then call a social worker, moron."

The social workers will say, "Fill in the forms first, you illiterate goon."

After they read the forms, they'll say, "Oh, in a well? Why didn't you say so? You think we have ladders, idiot? Call the fire department."

And there will always be some childish, personal feud involved like, "My mother-in-law works for them. The cow came fishing in our boat, took home the two biggest salmon, but wouldn't share in the gas costs. I don't speak to her."

Naarlanders.

I gave up on the harbour police with Sergeant Panigoniak. He walked us to within talking distance of Lundgren.

"Talk to him, please, Sir," the sergeant said to me. "Calm him."

I cleared my throat. "Lundgren, you pig. I have a hen to pluck with you."

The sergeant looked shocked. Lundgren looked surprised.

"Per, is that you?" said Lundgren.

"Ja, ja. Me. Are you going to pay me before you jump?"

"What?" said the sergeant.

"Pay you what?" said Lundgren, swaying back and forth on the parapet.

"Lundgren, you tightwad bastard, you owe me 32 dollars from our last poker game. Were you going to jump without paying your debts?"

"Per, I don't pay money to card cheats. You're a real Nils, you."

The sergeant was trying to shush me, but I was annoyed. A cheat? And a Nils? I don't know who the original Nils was or what he did, but if you want to start a brawl in a Naarlen bar, just call someone a Nils.

"You're a tightwad, Lundgren and a lousy loser. If you're not going to pay, just jump. Make the world a better place."

"Don't call me a tightwad, you cheat, you."

"Sir, better you be quiet now..."

"I will not be quiet, Mr. Policeman. Lundgren, come here and call me a cheat and a Nils and I'll rip your ears off."

"Shush, Sir, please, you're not helping by..."

Lundgren was bouncing up and down on the parapet, oblivious of the drop.

"Per, call me a tightwad again, I'll kick your ass, I don't care how many policemen you've brought to help you."

"Gentlemen, please, this is no way..."

"Tightwad, tightwad. Tightwad. Where is my 32 dollars?"

"Card cheat, card cheat, card cheat."

The sergeant was trying to calm us both, but he'd lost control of the discussion.

"You're the only Nils here, Lundgren."

Lundgren was red in the face. He climbed off the parapet, supposedly to kick my ass. He put down his shopping bag, rolled up his raincoat sleeves and came running at me. He swung his arms wildly, his fists bunched, his flip-flops flopping.

The sergeant stepped between us saying once more, "Gentlemen, please, this is no way..."

Lundgren's fist caught him in the ribs. A mistake—the swing was meant for me.

My shoe caught the sergeant in the rear—only a partial mistake, but I hoped it would look like one. I was still browned off at the Naarlen police. Particularly Mr. Three-Stripes-and-a-Crown, the Russian who called in the sex crimes unit.

I shouted "tightwad" again, hoping to see Lundgren swing at the sergeant one more time. It's what I call a win-win situation.

Unfortunately, Lundgren was no match for the efficient Sergeant Panigoniak. He had already cuffed Lundgren and was bundling him into the police cruiser. In all the excitement, I don't think the sergeant had yet registered my nudge to his rear end. He eased himself into the driver's seat.

I said to him, "Hey, what about me?"

The sergeant shook his head. "Can't give rides to civilians while transporting prisoners."

Then he roared off. It made me wonder if he perhaps he *had* noticed the kick in the bum. I started to walk away. A bystander, one of the bridge repair crew, handed me Lundgren's shopping bag saying, "You can't leave this here."

I was too tired to argue. An unusual state for me, I admit. Maybe because I didn't take a meal with the dog pills. I meekly took Lundgren's shopping bag from the man and went to find my parked ute. It was too late now for the bank. And since I still had no cash, it was no go for the milk either. I gave up and drove home. I parked the ute on our driveway, plugged in the block heater, grabbed my keys and Lundgren's shopping bag and got ready for my next battle.

Inge was standing inside the door waiting for me.

I looked at her warily. She gave me a huge hug and a smile.

"I'm sorry I was grumpy this morning. I had a sleep this afternoon and feel much better."

She grabbed Lundgren's shopping bag and dug through the contents making little "oohs."

"Croissants. How nice. And a cheese cake. You've never bought us cheese cake before, I love it."

I debated telling her it was not my shopping, but nixed that thought. She was still digging through Lundgren's bag.

"Oh, Per," she said with a big smile.

She lifted a two-litre carton of milk out of the shopping bag, put it back into the bag. Then she enveloped me in another hug, a huge kiss, and took my hand.

"Come sit with me."

We walked into the living room, hand in hand. Her hand was warm against mine. The feel was electric. I gazed sideways at her as we walked. Her beauty was as stunning as ever, even after all these years. My knees were rubber.

I said to myself, "You're one lucky guy, Per Pederson."

"I don't know what you got up to today," she said, "but there were so many phone messages for you while you were out. Some of them quite odd. I'm dying to know what they were about."

"Oh, ja?"

"First, Aarne left a message saying thanks for taking Magnus to the vet. He says the dog is much better now and he's very grateful. He is sorry he forgot to ask for your brown jacket. He says you must bring it to him please."

"Aha. Ja. Ha. Aarne. Ja, ja."

She gave my arm a squeeze. "

You're such a good man, Per."

I know this, of course, but, modestly, I made no comment. Still, it was nice to hear her say it.

She continued.

"Then the manager of the Naarlen and General Savings Co-op called. He wants to thank you for your part in preventing a ... a robbery. Is that right? A robbery? I hope you weren't in danger, Per? He says there will be an award dinner and a reward for you. And we're both invited to the dinner. You must tell me what that is about."

"Oh, ja, hm, the bank, that's nice, a dinner, ja, ja."

"And Mrs. Lundgren left a message. It seems her husband was a little confused today, poor man, and you were able to help him. She sounds very grateful."

"Oh, ja, Lundgren, that's right, ha. Lundgren, a bit confused, he was, definitely, ja."

"Mrs. Lundgren says it happens when he doesn't follow the instructions for his medication."

"Ja, ja. That's not good. Nei, nei, not good."

Inge gazed at me adoringly: the Batman of Naarlen, fighting crime and doing good on every street corner.

I wanted to ask, "Lundgren has ugly toes. He was wearing sandals. Do you think, Inge, people with toes like that should wear sandals?"

I value Inge's opinion on these types of issues. She was already telling me about another call, though.

"That is not all. A Sergeant Panigoniak called to say he was very impressed with the psychology you used on Mr. Lundgren. The sergeant says, 'thank you.' Wait now, I have it. He didn't say 'psychology'; he said, 'reverse psychology.'"

I briefly felt badly about trying to kick the man. Of course, the kick was my reaction to the Russian sergeant, not to the good Sergeant Panigoniak.

What is it that lawyers say? "Mens rea."

The intention defines the crime. My kick was intended for the Russian sergeant, so, even in law, it didn't count. I feel better about it.

"Oh, ja. Sergeant Panigoniak. A good man. So, he thanked me? That's good. Ja, ja. Definitely, good."

Inge cuddled into my side fondly.

"My hero," she said.

It was a bit muffled because her face was in my shoulder. I stroked her hair. Of course, she was right; all types of Naarlanders rely on me. They'd be lost without me. Not just the Batman of Naarlen, nei. The Batman and Robin of Naarlen, all in one, both at once. I smiled at the idea. I puffed out my chest.

Naarlen. My town, my Naarlanders, my people. There's no one like them. I love these people.

*

2. The Anniversary

So, the bank gave the big dinner for all of us. They fêted that stupid Grandma Mac, me and the idiot Russian police sergeant as heroes for thwarting the robbery. It was a full house, spouses and families invited. Inge, my wife, was chuffed, except ... well I'll come to the except later ... but that's women for you, there's always something.

The Russian's name turned out to be Mikhael Mikhaelovich Vasiliev. He, Grandma Mac and I were called to sit up on stage while the Naarlen and General Savings Co-op manager gave a speech about our (mainly my) heroism. The Russian was called up first, then Grandma Mac, then me. As I walked up to the stage to join them, the Russian made a V with two fingers, pointed it at his eyes, then pointed it at my eyes and mouthed "Pervert." He still believed there was something between me and Aarne's dog.

I had to squeeze past him to get to my seat on stage. There wasn't much room and I may have accidentally stood on his foot. He yelped. I jumped back in concern and spilled some water from my glass onto his lap.

"Sorry Mikhaelova," I said, squeezing by and hastily sitting down in my chair.

All in all, it was a good evening, especially watching the sergeant stand up in the crowded hall to shake the bank manager's hand. We all pretended not to see the dark stain on his lap.

"Fear of public speaking," I whispered to the bank manager.

After the big dinner, Inge and I walked home with Inge strutting like a peahen (if peahens strut). The downside came later. The Naarlen Herald (*"Our Community's Voice in the Arctic")* printed a very flattering photo of me. I began to get fan mail, particularly from some very nice young women.

Inge confronted me at breakfast with a few of these letters. They'd been addressed to me, but she'd opened them.

"This has to stop, Per."

She was waving an envelope that had purple hearts printed around the border.

Did she mean that she had to stop opening my mail? That sounded like a reasonable assumption, but I've learned with Inge to test my assumptions.

"What has to stop, sweetheart, mine?"

"These women have to stop writing to you."

"Very well, dear. Give me the addresses, I'll visit them and explain your request."

Apparently, this was not what she had in mind either.

"Look at this letter, Per. There's some simpering dolt of a giddy adolescent that says she's added a padlock to the side of the harbour bridge with your and her name on the padlock."

"A padlock? Why, for heaven's sake?"

"Don't you know anything? It's all the rage among teenage courting couples. You lock a padlock with both your initials to the bridge as a sign of your enduring love."

This was news to me. The world has evolved since my teenagedom, but this seemed like a good idea.

"I suppose it's more ecological than carving initials on tree trunks. That can't be good for trees, can it, Inge?"

Again, this was not well received.

The temperature in our household remained chilly until Saturday. Our anniversary. We had a lovely brunch at the Narwhal's Tooth.

At the end of brunch, I said, "How about I get the car from round back. You wait here. Linger over your coffee and meet me outside in ten. That will give me time to walk down to the harbour bridge and cut off the stupid padlock that's been bothering you."

"Cut off? How?"

"I put my bolt cutters in the back of the car, just for this."

"Good. Get rid of that thing, and I'll meet you outside in ten minutes."

At the harbour bridge, I was hunting through scores of padlocks when I heard my name being called from the quay below.

"Per, down here, please. Quickly."

Is it just me or do any of you find that the world's an odd place? Until the bank dinner, I hadn't seen any of Naarlen's police in weeks, and now, here was the other police sergeant that I knew, David Panigoniak, hailing me. He was holding up a very drunken, large, dishevelled woman.

"Come quickly, Per."

Unlike Mikhail Mikhailovich, I like David. He's the one solid, reliable, straight-shooting member of the Naarlen police force. I trotted down to the quay.

"David."

"Are those bolt cutters, Per?"

"Ja, ja, bolt cutters."

"Then come with me please."

We walked over to a harbour police launch.

"Here," said David, "you hold Edna upright. Pass her to me when I'm onboard."

"Good. Now you climb on. Right. Now, please, see the padlock blocking the wheelhouse door? I need you to cut that."

"Err ... what's happening David?"

He laid Edna out on the deck. She snored.

"Per, the Mafia twins have stolen old Nolan's rowboat and disappeared out of the harbour with it."

He meant the Garibaldi boys. They were about twelve years old and notorious for stunts like this.

"So?"

"Bad storm coming, Per. They're in big danger. Keep working at that padlock, it's almost cut through."

"Why am I cutting this lock? Why don't the harbour police unlock it and look for the twins?"

"Per, I explained this last time. The harbour police hate us regular police. They wouldn't piss on us in a fire."

"Oh, for heaven's sake, David, give me your cell, mine's in the car."

I grabbed his cell and dialled 922—our Naarlen harbour police.

A pleasant woman's voice: "Harbour Police Dispatch. How may we help?"

"Ja, ja, this is Per Pederson, I'm..."

"Wait a moment. You think I don't have call display? It's you again, David. I don't know what you're trying to pull, but you can suck my dick. And the seal meat in the freezer is mine. I never said I'd share it with your mother."

She hung up.

David looked at me. "My aunt. It's hopeless."

"I don't think your aunt understands what "suck my dick" means."

"Just finish cutting that padlock."

"What about the drunk?"

"Edna. No time to take her back to the station. Storm's coming fast. Stand by Edna in case she wakes up. Hold her down if she does. Don't want her going overboard."

He fussed with the mooring lines, woke up the diesels, fussed with some levers and knobs then said.

"Right. Let's go save the Mafia."

The engines roared, the quay moved away from us.

"David! My wife is expecting me..."

"You want to be on time for your wife but let two boys drown...?"

He gave me a long look. I shrugged. David has an unanswerable long look. I wish I could do those, but I can't.

By then we were in open water, outside the harbour break wall. I staggered. The swells were huge.

"Where are you going to look for them?"

"What?"

Diesel and storm-force winds were making talking difficult.

"WHERE WILL YOU LOOK FOR THEM?"

"Seal island. That's where I'd fish if I were twelve years old in a stolen row boat. Trouble is the rocks around the island are a death trap once the waves get stirred up. And the island will be underwater soon. Tide's coming in."

Seal Island came into view quickly. David throttled back to assess.

"We may be too late to get through. Look how the rocks are throwing waves across the gap."

I looked.

"Jesus, Mary, Joseph and the little donkey too," I said, "will you look at that?"

When the waves hit the rocks, the spray was going up thirty feet. And when the waves pulled back, about twenty feet of black sharp-edged rocks showed. Then another wave would obscure them in a welter of white. Putting a boat near those would be suicide.

"Here," said David, "hold the wheel steady like so. Right. Now if the waves push us back, you give a little more gas on this lever, like so. Just to hold position. But for God's sake DON'T move us forward. We can't move in until I've figured out how to do this safely. Killing ourselves won't help rescue the boys."

He moved forward to the bow to survey the situation. He stood there, staring hard. Then he pointed to our right, shouting, "Point us that way, but don't move (something, something)."

It was almost impossible to hear him.

"Don't WHAT, David?"

"Don't move (something, something)."

"Don't move WHAT, David?"

"FORWARD."

The man was raving mad. I couldn't have understood him, could I?

"What?"

"FORWARD."

Jaevlig satan. I shut my eyes and rammed the throttle forward, just as a large wave lifted us. I couldn't bear to look. Damn David. I hate the whole Naarlen police force. There was a bang, a scrape, a welter of spray, we were rising, spinning and then (I peeked) the wave threw us *over* a giant rock and into the relative calm on the far side. We dropped with a thump. I fell down. When I dared look next, the sergeant was standing over me

"Was that skill Per? Or should I shoot you for that mad dog caper? And for disobeying orders? I told you FIVE times not to move forward."

He was furious. I wanted to argue the point about disobeying orders, but had the strange sensation that my bowels were connected to my vocal chords, and that if I opened one, I'd open both. I shut my mouth. Tight.

He held out his hand to help me stand. I looked around. We had been magically transported inside the ring of rocks. In the relative calm, we were nudging Seal Island with our bow. Two very relieved looking little boys were staring at us from the island.

David waved to them. "I'll get them and the damned rowboat on board. Then we should get out of here before the storm arrives."

"God help us," I thought to myself, "This isn't the storm yet?"

I spent the trip back in sheer terror. David offered to let me steer us out of the ring of rocks. He still thought I might be a hotshot.

I feigned nonchalance, "Nei, nei, David. Going out will be much easier than coming in. I'll let you do it. Good practice for you."

I shut my eyes, gripped the railings tight and my bowels even tighter. The boat bounced like a rodeo bull.

I prayed:

"Dear God, David Panigoniak, is a good man, willing to sacrifice himself... and me and Edna, thoughtless bastard and *dtrittsek* that he is... Nei, nei, scratch that last part and let's try again... David Panigoniak is a good man trying to save everyone. Please recognize his goodness and get me... I mean 'us'—after all there are children involved, and although I'm not partial to them it's said that you are ... please get us out of this mess in one piece, and with my trousers unsullied. I know I haven't..."

"You're still watching Edna are you, Per?"

"Ja, ja, of course, David."

I opened my eyes. It seemed we were through the ring of rocks and still alive. I'd gotten us in by sheer luck, surfing a big wave, and misunderstanding his order. David, it seemed, had gotten us out by sheer skill and calm calculation.

"Just, I thought maybe you'd nodded off, Per."

"Nei, nei, I'm watching her. Just shut my eyes against the salt for a moment."

"That was as big a wave as I ever want to go through. Wouldn't like to do that more than once a day, Per."

"Ja, ja, nei, nei."

"Listen, Per," said David as we approached the harbour, "not a word to anyone about this, please."

"Why?"

"If word gets out that the Mafia twins stole a boat it will be reform school down south for them. I'd like to spare them that if I can. Plus, criminal charges for you—breaking the lock on a police boat."

"What!!"

"For sure. I'd have to testify. You cut the lock."

I was enraged. That fucking Panigoniak. *Fittetryne.* I hate the man. He'd make a corkscrew look straight. I intend to send his aunt flowers and lengthy suggestions for what to do with her nephew.

I was still seething when we tied up to the dock. He tied the mooring lines and shooed the twins. They set off towing Old Nolan's row boat back to its normal mooring.

"I'll get out first, Per. You hand me Edna... There... Right... Help me walk her up to the police car, I have to book her for drunk and disorderly."

We arrived at the cruiser.

"You hold her up, Per," he said while searching for his keys.

Edna stirred and put her arms around me.

"Ello, loverboy. Wann'a drink?"

She nuzzled my neck. Her breath smelled of cheap wine and free puke.

"That must 'ave been one 'ell of a night. I swear I felt the ground move under me for a while back there. Doesn't usually happen like that. Did it move for you too?"

I looked up the hill towards the Narwhal's Tooth. Was that Inge up there staring at us? Squinting to decide whether that really was me.

"Er... Not now please, Edna."

"A shy one. I like that."

Her arms clamped tighter.

"Gi' us a kiss then."

"No."

Damn it, it was Inge, and she was walking closer. She still wasn't sure it was me, but the distance was narrowing rapidly.

"Jus' a little one."

"No. Let go."

The sergeant got her off me and put her into the cruiser. Inge was even closer. I had only seconds before Inge confirmed recognition.

"David, put me in the cruiser too. Quickly."

"Can't put civilians in with a prisoner."

Desperate times, desperate measures: I kicked his shins, hard, and then smacked his face as he bent to clutch his legs.

Panigoniak may be a bastard, but he's efficient. In no time flat, I was cuffed and on the back seat next to Edna.

Inge was within ID range. I ducked my head below the seatback.

David started the engine and eased the car slowly up the hill to pass Inge.

All would have been well. Except. Edna. She pulled my head up, cuddled my head on her shoulder and said, "I still fancy you, sweetheart."

Then she puked on me.

And that fucking Panigoniak. He recognized Inge and stopped the car.

"I have to book him. If you want to bail him out, come down in half an hour."

Inge peered through the window at me. And at Edna.

"No," she said, "I don't think I will. You and the ... lady ... next to him are welcome to him."

She turned and left.

*

3. The Bridge

Naarlen's history surprises most people. It was Germany's only colonial Arctic possession until the end of World War I. Under the Treaty of Versailles, after that war, it became a League of Nations mandate governed by Canada. You'd think ancient history like that wouldn't matter these days, but you'd be wrong. I'll explain, but first let me take you back to my arrest.

Things took a while to return to normal. Inge was furious with me for several days. Sergeant Panigoniak, that heart of gold, eventually forgave my assault and explained things to Inge. I gave Panigoniak dried seal meat, to make up for the assault, and we were good again. He still thinks I piloted the police boat across the waves and rocks by skill and nerve. I didn't. He did. We have huge respect for each other. The difference is his respect for me is founded on a misunderstanding, my respect for him is well grounded.

Edna sobered up and apologized to Inge. She's quite likeable when not on a bender—I mean Edna is quite likeable, not Inge. Damn, that came out wrong.

Inge is likeable too, obviously, when she's not mad at me, but I meant Edna was the one who'd been on a bender, not Inge.

Inge's reconciliation with me got a lift when I agreed that our old carpet needed replacing.

"You'll arrange for new hardwood flooring, then, Per?"

"I'll get right on it."

Garibaldi Senior, the father of the Mafia twins, came by to thank me for rescuing the twins. That kicked off a new chain of events. Garibaldi Senior spotted a house for sale behind our property, bought it, and moved in. My new neighbours. The Mafia twins and I get on well, despite their evil reputation. They too were awed by how I skillfully piloted the police launch to rescue them. Once again, respect founded on a misunderstanding.

Our two houses share a common garden fence. The Garibaldi family kept hens in their back yard. About once a week, one would escape into our yard. Inge alerted me whenever that happened.

"Per! There's a hen in our garden!"

I'd pick up the bird, put it into a cardboard box, close the lid to calm the animal, then carry it around to the Garibaldi's front door. It was no bother, and they always gave me fresh eggs.

You'll recall The Narwhal's Tooth, the lovely French restaurant by the harbour where Inge and I celebrated our anniversary just before the incident with Edna and the Mafia twins? Naarlen also has an establishment called The Narwhal's ***Other*** Tooth. Not a restaurant, not French, and not even distantly related to the word "lovely."

The Other Tooth is a bar run by Bernhard Halloran, an Aussie. The bar has sawdust on the floor, serves beer, pork rinds, peanuts, fish and chips, pizza and more beer. The TV shows ancient videos of Australian rugby and cricket matches.

Why Bernie chose the Arctic instead of sunning himself on Bondi Beach in Sydney is a mystery. Henri at the real Narwhal's Tooth says it's because Bernie was facing jail time in Oz for immoral relations with a kangaroo.

Whatever his reason for leaving Oz, Bernie's arrival was Naarlen's gain. Besides running the unlovely, but ever-popular Other Tooth, Bernie is Naarlen's mayor, a consummate politician, and as sharp a shark as you hope never to run into.

Take happy hour at the Other Tooth on Friday afternoons. The pub is overflowing. Beer is free during Happy Hour at The Other Tooth. Yes, you heard it right. Free.

The catch is pure Bernie genius: free beer, but thirty dollars each time you use the urinal. And, not coincidentally, the first thing Bernie did as mayor, was to increase the fines for public urination in the streets of Naarlen.

The miners who gulp beer at The Other Tooth on Friday afternoons always underestimate how much "free" beer they'll drink, and overestimate how long they can hold it in. There are a few lucky winners, but like any casino, the odds favour the house. Women get both free beer and free washroom usage during happy hour. That draws even more men to Bernie's "free" beer casino. Again, pure genius.

I once asked Bernie how he came up with such ideas.

His answer was cryptic. "Per, me mate," he said, "if you want to sell 'em myxomatosis, you've first got to sell 'em the rabbits."

There are linear thinkers like me—every step laid out clearly and following logically from the previous one. There are intuitive thinkers like Inge—linear thinkers who only show you every fifth step of their logic. And then, there are thinkers like Bernie who think around corners.

Look at what happened with Naarlen's old wooden harbour bridge. The bridge needed replacing, and the costs for a new, modern bridge were crippling. Naarlen council was stuck. They wanted a bridge. They didn't want to spend the money.

"Leave it to me," Mayor Bernie told the councillors.

The next week he announced that Naarlen was twinning with Ostermark, a small town near Berlin, Germany.

The council grumbled. "We don't have enough money for a bridge and Bernie's burning dollar bills to fly back and forth to Germany? Worse still, he's flying in German diplomats and reporters into Naarlen on our dime? He's gone mad."

They grumbled but they couldn't figure out what to do about Bernie. He's always been careful to persuade only the most ineffectual citizens to run for council. It gives him more room for unfettered action. Bernie ignored his council. Instead, he wined and dined the foreign visitors and organized tours of Naarlen for them.

He asked me if I would be tour guide for a Herr Schmidt, the mayor of our now twin city, Ostermark.

"Sure, Bernie. What should I show him?"

"Per, show him the seal colony, or the snow geese rookery, or take him fishing. Whatever."

Herr Schmidt was a surprise. Did he want to see the seal breeding colony?

"No, no." Long pause. "No zeals. No dunk you, Herr Pederzohn."

His English is far better than my German, but Schmidt was born in Saxony. Saxons talk like that even in German.

"Would you like to go out on the water fishing for salmon or watching whales, Herr Schmidt?"

"No, no. Nod boatz." Long pause. "No, no. No dunk you, Herr Pederzohn."

"What would you like to see, Herr Schmidt?"

"Two dingz, bleaze Herr Pederzohn. I much like your high school do zee, and I much like Herr Halloranz bar do zee."

Herr Schmidt spent an hour chatting to Lundgren, the principal of the high school. I sat at the table with them and nodded off in boredom. After that, Herr Schmidt and I went to The Other Tooth. It was Friday afternoon. I explained the "free beer" concept to Herr Schmidt. I thought he'd be surprised.

"Och ja," he said. "In Chermany, vee know diss from old. Zuch a stubid drick."

Being a visiting dignitary, he got both free beer and free toilet usage. He tried a Nova Scotia pale ale and liked it. He tried the urinal and said German urinals were better.

At the Friday night dinner in the Naarlen town hall, Bernie sat next to a German State Secretary for Foreign Affairs ("Staatssekretär im Auswertigen Amt") and chatted to him about Naarlen's German heritage.

"Wouldn't it be good, Herr Staatssekretär, to name something important in Naarlen to reflect our fascinating German colonial past?" said Bernie after the State Secretary's third champagne.

"Like what?" said the secretary, intrigued.

You can see where Bernie was taking this. After the foreign visitors flew home, Bernie addressed council.

"I'm happy to report that Germany will design, build and pay for our new harbour bridge. It will be completed without a dime of Naarlen money. In return it will be known as the Chancellor Willy Brandt Bridge, in honour of Germany's fourth post-war chancellor, and in honour of Germany's historic ties with Naarlen."

The councillors were dumbfounded.

"No Naarlen tax money at all?"

"Not a single cent."

"And it will be a modern bridge—concrete, two lanes?"

"Concrete and steel. Two lanes. The best of German engineering."

"When will we have it?"

"It will be ready in six months."

"Guaranteed?"

"Guaranteed."

When Bernie appeared before council back then to announce the German funding for the new bridge, he looked embarrassed, though. The councillors cheered and cheered. Bernie had to wave them to a stop.

"There was one tiny quid pro quo that the German State Secretary demanded," he said.

"What?" asked the councillors.

Bernie looked more embarrassed.

"A trifle, really."

"What?" repeated the councillors.

"Actually, it was the mayor of our twin city, Ostermark, who demanded it."

"What?" demanded the councillors more sharply. They're fools—carefully selected by Bernie—but they're not total fools.

Bernie cleared his throat. "The Mayor of Ostermark, a Herr Schmidt, which I think is German for smith, or farrier, if you will, an ancient profession and..."

"What did you agree to?" said the councillors.

"Herr Schmidt suggested that beyond inanimate infrastructure objects like a bridge, we should have more human ... more personal ties between Naarlen and Germany. I could hardly refuse."

The councillors stared uneasily.

"Herr Schmidt found out that we have an opening for a high school English teacher in Naarlen. Some mindless idiot here in Naarlen, some mindless idiot who should have kept his mouth shut, revealed this to Herr Schmidt."

Bernie scanned the audience looking for the offending idiot. He didn't notice me in the audience. In any case, he meant Lundgren, the principal at the high school.

Then he continued, "Herr Schmidt suggested that we offer a one-year contract to one of Ostermark's English teachers, a Herr Eberhardt Kritzinger."

"A German to teach English?"

"Herr Kritzinger is apparently very well qualified." Bernie sounded defensive. A rare state for Bernie.

"We should interview him," said a councillor.

"To what end?" said Bernie impatiently. The fool of the councillor had not yet grasped the situation. "If you like him, the interview is a waste of time."

"And if we don't like him?"

"You'll take him anyway, or lose the free bridge."

"What's this teacher done that they need to send him to Naarlen?" asked a second councillor. "Do they have Kangaroos in Germany?"

Bernie ignored that. He controls who becomes councillor as best he can, but sometimes a smartass slips through. Democracy is a slippery beast to control.

"Probably he just murdered a student," said a third glumly.

"Or two, or three," said a fourth.

"Come, come. Ladies, Gentlemen, Councillors," said Bernie, regaining his poise, now that he'd admitted the worst. "We can spare a student or two. We might like this one or that one, but en-mass they're a nuisance. In the unlikely event that Herr Kritzinger murders one or two, then we have grounds to send him back AFTER the bridge is installed. And still keep the bridge."

The logic was unanswerable.

I had a private chat with Bernie the next morning, in The Other Tooth.

We drank a coffee together. Bernie and I are the only people in The Tooth who drink coffee, and I'm the only one of us who takes sugar. That explains why the sugar comes straight out of an almost full two-kilogram, rumpled paper sugar bag that looks like it's ten years old.

"Sounds like Herr Schmidt knows how to sell myxomatosis," I said.

Bernie spat into the sawdust. "Herr Schmidt is a scheming bastard of the first order. Do you know, Per, what Herr Schmidt's profession is, when he's not playing at mayor?"

"No. What?"

"He runs a beer garden."

"Oh, yes?"

"And did you know, his pub has the same happy Friday system as I do here?"

"Does it?"

"Oh, yes. And the canny swine knows that if you want free bridges, you have to take his reject teachers. I hate people like that. Don't you, Per?"

I made a noncommittal grunt.

"Who told Herr Schmidt about our vacant teacher position, Per."

"Lundgren, our high school principal."

"Isn't he the guy you stopped from jumping off the old harbour bridge?"

Bernie knows everything that goes on in Naarlen.

"Yes."

"Should have let him jump, Per."

"Too late, Bernie."

"Well, couldn't you stop him blabbing to Herr Schmidt about vacant teacher positions?"

"How, Bernie?"

"You could have kicked him under the table while the three of you were sitting chatting."

"Wish I had. He called me a 'Nils' once."

The idea of kicking Lundgren under the table took hold of me after that. He still hadn't paid his poker debt to me. I sauntered over to the school and asked the secretary if I could have five minutes of Lundgren's time.

The secretary, Jane Hennerman, is a lovely lady. She and I get on famously. She ushered me to a meeting room, brought me a coffee and said, "Just a moment. I'll fetch him. I always enjoy it when you meet with Mr. Lundgren. Is it still about his poker debts? No? I don't have to tell him. I'll let it be a surprise for him."

Lundgren came in holding his own still-steaming coffee mug and sat opposite me.

"Oh, it's you Per."

I kicked him under the table. He spilled his coffee onto his lap, yipped like a chihuahua, then hopscotched around the room shouting "*jävla idiot*", "*sabla skit*", and "*du satans helvetes förbannade jävla fan*," all the while holding his ankle with one hand and his lap with the other.

I stepped out and called Jane.

"I think Mr. Lundgren's having a fit of some kind. Can you see to him? I'll come back when he's feeling better."

"Of course, Per. Always a joy to have you interrupt our little daily routine. Regards to Inge."

I left feeling much better. It's funny how most people in Naarlen—people like Jane Hennerman, and the Mafia twins, and Sergeant Panigoniak, and the bank manager at the Standard Naarlen and General Savings Co-op, and the women who write me such nice cards and such—think I'm a swell guy and a hero, and yet Lundgren gets on with no one. Wouldn't it be wonderful if I could help him see his faults and change? Per Pederson, superhero interventionist. I sighed. Some things, I had to admit, were beyond even my skills.

Whatever the Ostermark teacher, Herr Kritzinger, had done to deserve banishment to Naarlen, he turned out to be a reasonable English teacher. He was much younger than I expected, late twenties perhaps, and a quiet, serious man. He had a tendency to pronounce his double-yous as vees and some of his single esses became double esses, but no one cared. He deviated from the Canadian syllabus by refusing to teach Shakespeare or Milton. Instead, he taught translations of Goethe and Schiller. Since most Naarlen high school students didn't give a damn for either Shakespeare, Milton, Goethe or Schiller, it didn't matter. What did matter to them was that he was a great soccer coach for the boys and a great volleyball coach for the girls.

All this blah blah about Mafia hens coming into our back yard, bridges, Bernie and Eberhardt Kritzinger is history. It would be water under the Willy Brandt Bridge, except that it set up the situation with Christine Nguyen and all that followed at the school board.

I'm on the Naarlen school board of trustees, so I know about the Christine Nguyen saga. It started just a few weeks after Eberhardt Kritzinger came to Naarlen High. Christine sent an application to our board. She was finishing her teacher certification. To complete, she needed to spend several months teaching under supervision. She applied to Naarlen High, in hopes of both gaining that teaching experience and also seeing Canada's high Arctic.

Bernie Halloran, our mayor, is head of the school board. I sat with him at The Other Tooth, sipping coffee and reviewing Christine's application.

"Refill, Per?"

"Please, Bernie."

He poured us each another cup and pushed over the ancient, almost full, two-kg pack of sugar to me. I took my half-teaspoon, closed the near-full bag and pushed it back. He put it under the counter, and said, "Her credentials are good."

"And her references are great."

"She wants to teach English, or history, or art and music."

"Very versatile, Bernie. And the English will come in handy when Eberhardt Kritzinger goes back to Germany. At the end of his year."

"We need to keep Eberhardt, Per."

"Why? We have the new German bridge. It's already open. Opened ahead of schedule. Paid for and all. We no longer need Eberhardt, Bernie."

"We need him."

"What? The bridge is no good, Bernie?"

"The bridge is magnificent, Per. But."

"But?"

"But the Germans engineers say the bridge needs to be checked after its first, fifth and tenth year of use. To ensure that it has settled in as intended without sagging, tilting or corrosion."

"Is that a problem, Bernie?"

"Bridge inspections are expensive. So, I've made a bet with Herr Schmidt."

"The Mayor of Ostermark, our twin city?

"Yes. If I can keep Kritzinger here an extra year, Ostermark Council has to pay for our bridge inspections."

"And the other side of the bet?"

"If Kritzinger goes back after his first year with us, we have to pay for renovations to the Ostermark Council chambers."

"Kritzinger wants to go back to Germany?"

"Yes, Per, damn him. As soon as his year's up."

"Pity. He's a good teacher."

"Yes, he is. More importantly, when he goes back, Naarlen has to pay for bridge maintenance AND Ostermark Council chamber renovations."

"Oof. Why is Herr Schmidt so keen to get rid of Kritzinger, Bernie?"

"Kritzinger comes from humble stock, but was romancing the daughter of one of the richest families in Ostermark. The girl's parents were unhappy."

"And the Mayor of Ostermark cares because?"

"Because the girl's family funds the mayor's campaigns."

"Ouch."

"Anyway, leave that to me, Per. I'll think of something. Now what about this Christine woman?"

"The board of trustees will want to do a video interview, before deciding."

"Can you set it up, Per? Line up the date with my office, I'd like to be in on the interview."

"Sure."

There are twelve school board members—five men and seven women—including Bernie and myself. We all attended the video interview.

The interview lasted an hour. Christine was even more impressive on live video than on her resumé. I'd guess she was about twenty-one. She oozed youth, enthusiasm, determination, charm, character and seemed artlessly unaware of how absolutely beautiful she was. The male trustees—no matter how ancient—fell under her spell, instantly. The women trustees, however, reacted with hostility.

Bernie told the trustees, "No need to decide immediately. Let's sleep on it and take a vote at the end of the week. Meanwhile, who wants to come down to my pub for some beer, pork rind fried in butter, country music and darts? Anyone?"

The women trustees declined. Which may have been what Bernie had intended.

He herded the male trustees into a quiet corner of the bar.

"Listen guys, I take it we'd all like to have this Christine as a student teacher? To inject some youth, enthusiasm, vitality and charm into Naarlen High? Something the school is lacking under Lundgren. He's a bureaucrat, not a leader."

The male trustees nodded. Unanimously.

Grampa Fergus said, "She reminds me of my daughter."

Our other ancient trustee, Grampa McVee, couldn't leave that alone. The two are forever at each other. Glasgow vs. Edinburgh or some such ancient rivalry.

"You don't have a daughter, Fergus."

"I have six sons."

"What's that got to do with you not having a daughter?"

"It's got everything to do with it. Why do you think I have six sons?"

"Why?"

"Because I kept trying for a daughter. I always wanted a daughter. And if I had a daughter, she'd be like Christine. Then Christine would remind me of my daughter. Can't you follow simple logic, McVee? What's wrong with you?"

Fergus wiped a tear of nostalgia for his daughter from his eyes.

"Oh, for heaven's sake, Fergus."

John Littleham, a bachelor at fifty-nine years old, interrupted this, "Grampa, if you had a daughter like that, I'd be camped in your kitchen every night."

"No, you wouldn't. You're not good enough for my daughter. Won't have you in my kitchen or anywhere near Christine."

For once, McVee took Fergus's side.

"And you're triple her age, you pervert. I wouldn't let you in my kitchen either. And, Fergus, while we're at it, how could she remind you of your daughter? Nguyen is a Vietnamese name."

"There are plenty of Nguyens in Scotland. Especially in Aberdeen."

"Aberdeen doesn't count. It's full of foreign oil companies."

"Your memory is going, is it, McVee? A Nguyen played on the Scottish curling team a few years back."

"An Aberdeen foreigner, then."

"No, no, McVee. Do you no' know anything? You have to be born in Scotland to play on the Scottish curling team. It's football that is full of foreigners: Italians, Argentines, even English. I mind the time we had a Dutchman, born in Barcelona, who played in goal for Kilmarnock. Was a useless git, too."

"Fergus, now whose memory is going? You mean he was Spanish? How can a Dutchman be born in Barcelona?"

"His parents were both from Rotterdam, on holiday in Barcelona when the wee man was born prematurely. An emergency C-section. That's how, you handless teuchter, you."

Bernie cut through the chit-chat.

"Gents. Councillors. Back to business please. We agree Christine would be a breath of fresh air for the school and Naarlen. Here's the thing. Christine is young, charming and beautiful, so the women trustees are nervous. Christine is a threat. For them, voting for Christine would be like voting the fox into the hen house. They're not going to do it. Unless you vote how I tell you."

"How's that, Bernie?"

"Well, the discussion ahead of the vote and the vote itself are different things, right? The discussion is an open forum that I chair. Everyone hears everyone else's opinions. The vote, though, is secret, by anonymous paper ballot. My secretary and I see the ballots to count them, but even my secretary and I don't know who voted which way."

"So? Whatever we say during the open discussion, Bernie, the women still outvote us. And we'll never persuade them."

"Right. So, here's what I need you to do."

He spent several minutes making sure we understood his instructions. Then he told us how firing squads work.

When I got home, Inge had been on the phone with my fellow school board trustee, Helen Meier.

"Helen says you interviewed a young student teacher today."

"That's right, Inge."

"A woman."

"I believe that's correct, Inge. I didn't pay attention."

"I hope you won't vote to bring her to Naarlen, Bernie. Helen says she's very unsuitable. Dresses far to fashionably for a teacher, plays on her looks, is too full of herself, and wasn't respectful of the trustees. Helen says a young woman like that would be a disruptive influence for the boys in the classroom, and for the men teachers at the school."

"Hmm. I'm sure you're right, Inge. Very disruptive. I can see that, now you mention it."

"So, I can tell Helen, you'll be voting against her application?"

"You've convinced me, Inge. Yes, I'll vote against."

I found out subsequently that every married male board member had gotten similar instructions from his wife. The female board members have an excellent network and tentacles into every household that the SAVAK, MOSSAD, CIA, KGB etc. could only dream of.

When the board reconvened to debate Christine's application, Bernie invited comments from all. The women held back to see if the men would follow their wives' instructions.

Grampa Fergus began. "In my day, teaching wasn't considered a fit job for women."

"True, Fergus," said McVee. "I mind the women teachers in my day. Nae sense of professionalism, just husband hunting. They had nae classroom control, nae sense of discipline, nae dedication. I doubt not it has'nae changed."

"Aye, this Christine woman, now, McVee. She'd probably be a'right teaching a girls' school..."

"Junior girls' school, Fergus. Or kindergarten."

"Right, McVee, but no' a co-ed high school. You need a man for that job. With a firm hand and discipline."

"Aye, and dedication to their profession. Not spouse hunting. In my day, women were governesses, kindergarten teachers or wet nurses."

The women board members were looking angry. Helen Meier spoke up.

"Bernie, I find this discussion distasteful. As it happens, I'm against Christine's application, but certainly not because she's a woman. A woman is quite capable of doing this work, and better than any man."

Bernie nodded and turned to me. "What do you think, Per?"

"Well, Bernie, I'm all for equal opportunity employment. I think we have some excellent women miners here in Naarlen, for example. We also have a woman dispatcher on the harbour police force, although I hear she never actually goes out on the boat."

Helen was getting red in the face and wanted to interrupt. Bernie held up a hand. "Please let Per finish. You'll get your chance afterwards."

I continued. "As I say, I'm all for equal opportunity. However, I have to be mindful of our constituents' wishes. I've heard from parents recently that hiring a young, attractive woman would be distracting to the male students and male teachers. I personally find this attitude one-sided, but as a school board trustee I have to listen to their wishes. So, I will vote against this woman teacher. Nothing against Christine. But if parents don't think a woman teacher is appropriate, I say we shouldn't take Christine."

Helen and the other women trustees were bursting with rage. They shouted at once.

"And what about men teachers distracting the female students and staff?"

"Male poppycock!"

"That is so insulting to women!"

"I'm going to vote to accept Christine just to demonstrate my faith in women as teachers!"

"Me too."

"And me."

"And me."

Bernie nodded politely. "Thank you, ladies. How about hearing from John Littleham? John?"

John cleared his throat. "I don't doubt that Christine has the ... theoretical ... qualifications. However, I looked at our high school results for the last five years. The top students have all been girls. Year in, year out. It's the boys that need most help. Christine—or any woman teacher—just wouldn't provide the role model that the boys—the students most in need of help—need. No, if we're taking on another teacher it needs to be a man."

The women were on their feet, raging.

Helen shouted, "Hold the vote now, Bernie. We women are voting for Christine."

Claudia Van Dam added, "And we don't care what antediluvian attitudes you chauvinists have. We have a majority vote. Christine will show you she's better than any male."

"Damn right," shouted Tracy Vickers. "And we'll give her all our help and support. We'll make sure she's the best teacher you've ever seen."

"Yes!!"

"Fem power rules."

"Right on, girl!"

"A woman needs a man..."

"... like a fish needs a bicycle."

"You tell 'em, Sister."

"Sisterhood forever!!"

There was further shouting from the women. Bernie held up his hands and passed out the secret ballots. When the vote was tallied, Christine's application had been approved eleven in favour, one against. The votes were, of course, anonymous. But we men knew a secret, because Bernie had planned it with us back at the pub. The secret that every man kept to himself was that Bernie had placed the sole voted against Christine.

At supper, I said to Inge, "You know, Bernie told me something interesting about firing squads."

"What's that Per?"

"Firing squads are typically made up of twelve riflemen. The officer gives eleven of them a real bullet and the twelfth gets a blank. No one knows who got the blank. That way after the execution, each rifleman can say to himself, 'It felt like a blank, I wasn't the executioner. My conscience is clear.'"

"Huh," said Inge. "What a useless piece of information. No application to our lives, thank goodness. More importantly did you vote against Christine today like I asked?"

"Of course, dear," I said. "Unfortunately, mine was the only vote against. All the other men voted for her."

She put her hand on mine. "No matter about the others. I knew I could count on you. I'm proud of you."

I had no doubt that every married male trustee was having the same discussion with his wife, and saying the same thing: "Yes, dear, I voted against. Just like you told me. I was the only one. But you asked and I did."

I began to sense why Bernie had to leave Australia. He was a threat to every other politician there. Who knows how high he could have climbed if they hadn't shipped him to Naarlen?

The love the women trustees felt for Christine vanished within two weeks of her arrival in Naarlen. That's when she appeared before the school board and demanded funds for her first project.

"A zoo?" said Helen Meier. "Why?"

"Because the students here have never touched or seen even the most common farm animals from down south. Never mind exotic animals."

"Tell me again," said Tracy Vickers, "what animals do you want to bring here?"

"A sheep, an alpaca, and a penguin. For starters."

"You've got goddamned gall," said Claudia van Dam. "You've been here just two weeks, you know nothing about our community or our northern values, and already you want to change us. Typical Southerner."

Claudia's always been aggressive. We call her Jean-Claudia.

Christine took it well. She didn't back down.

"It's precisely while I'm new that my view of you is clearest—before I accept your status quo. It's now that I can best see areas of difference or even improvement. I thought you'd welcome that."

"Hear, hear," said Grampa Fergus.

"Lots of sense in that," said McVee, a rare agreement with Fergus.

"Right on," said John Littleham, miserable brown-nosing git that he is.

The male support for Christine, plus the nagging feeling that they'd been railroaded in bringing her to Naarlen, annoyed the women even further.

"Way too expensive."

"Extravagant."

"Totally unnecessary."

"Who needs a zoo?"

"Think of all the good we could do with the money you want to waste on this ridiculous zoo," said Helen.

"Like what?" asked Christine.

It seemed a logical question to me, but annoyed Helen even more.

"That's for the board to decide, not you. Request denied."

"How can you deny the request without voting on it?" asked Christine.

"Fine," said Helen through gritted teeth. "We'll vote."

Votes on project budgets are not anonymous. The split was as expected. Four men in favour, seven women against. Bernie was absent on council business. Not that his vote would have changed anything.

Grampa Fergus leaned over to Christine and patted her shoulder. "Never fret, lassie. It's a grand idea, as anyone with half a brain should see. Talk to me after and we'll make it happen without the school board. Right?"

Christine thanked Gramps, thanked the board with a smile and left without any hint of dejection or animosity.

I had a private chat with Bernie after the board meeting. He was mildly surprised how quickly the women board members had turned against Christine.

"I expected it to take longer," he said.

"Oh well, you know what they say, Bernie: familiarity breeds, etc."

He looked at me thoughtfully, as though I had said something profound. "Does it, now?"

"Oh, yes, Bernie, everyone knows that."

"Per, Per, what would Naarlen do without you?"

While that's true, and nice of Bernie to recognize, I'm not sure why he brought it up just then. Still a compliment is a compliment and I accepted it without questioning him further.

What a whirlwind Christine was. Two weeks later she and her grade elevens had converted a disused fish farming facility into three animal pens: one cozy straw-lined pen for the alpaca, another for the lone sheep, and a concrete fish holding tank for the lone penguin. The fish farm was one of Grampa Fergus's early ventures. Unused in recent years, but still his. McVee, a big shareholder of Naarlen Airways, arranged for free airlift of the animals from down south. God knows where they found the penguin.

Penguins are South Pole beasts, not North Pole. The Naarlen Chamber of Commerce, mostly run by Bernie, Grampa Fergus and McVee, sponsored half the animal feed for the coming year. Cake sales, donations and raffles at the high school *and* junior school bought feed for the other half year. Both the junior and high school (minus the board) got behind the project. It was the talk of every school student and every family at dinner time for weeks.

The grand opening of the Naarlen Zoo was a huge success. It was hosted by the Grade Elevens and their parents. I doubt any family in Naarlen missed it. For a dollar a turn, the youngest visitors (seven and under) were allowed to feed handfuls of grain to the sheep or alpaca or toss sardines to the penguin. Naarlen's keenest gardeners placed orders for sheep and alpaca dung. For a more exorbitant fee, visitors aged eight and up could be honorary zoo keepers for a week, paying for the honour of cleaning out the pens and feeding the animals. The fleece crop (both alpaca and sheep) for the coming year was auctioned for a surprising amount of money to those who wanted to try their hand at wool carding and spinning.

And if you think that the zoo's opening success made the women school board trustees love Christine better, you need to get out more.

While Christine was winning the battle of the zoo, I was facing problems at home.

"Tell me again, Per, why have you delayed our new hardwood floor installation?"

"Hardwood shouldn't be installed with winter coming, Inge. The new floor needs to mature in a gentle climate after it's laid. In the spring, sweetheart mine. Be patient."

That's possibly true, no strike that, I'm sure I've heard that somewhere about wood floors. The real reason I was delaying the floor was more complicated.

Word of Bernie's bet with the Mayor of Ostermark, Herr Schmidt, had spread. John Littleham was taking side bets on whether Bernie would win or lose his bet with Herr Schmidt. Most of the punters thought Bernie had no chance of winning. Littleham was offering such long odds against Bernie that I had to take a position. Having seen how skillfully Bernie played the bridge funding and the women school board trustees, I put money on Bernie's success at keeping Kritzinger an extra year. I bet the hardwood floor budget. As soon as Bernie won his bet with Mayor Schmidt, Inge would get her new hardwood floor and I would have a large profit besides.

Don't get me wrong. I don't gamble. It's evil and addictive. It makes one rely on luck instead of skill and depresses the spirit. Look how miserable Lundgren is over his unpaid poker debts. He almost threw himself off a bridge once. And people kick him under the table. But this, this wasn't a gamble. It was an obvious investment. You just had to review Bernie's history and do the math on the odds John was offering to see that. Inge has no appreciation for finance, though, so it was easier to say the wood floor should be laid in gentler weather.

Trouble was, every time I dropped in on Bernie after that check on my investment, Bernie's mind was on something else.

"Kritzinger?" Bernie said to me. "Forget Kritzinger. It's Christine that's important."

Didn't he realize he'd won the battle against the women trustees already? He had to let go of that battle and move on to the current battle—the bet against Schmidt and for keeping Kritzinger.

Each time he said "Forget Kritzinger," he reminded me of one of those old cavalry generals who went into WWI with troops on horseback charging tanks and machine guns. The once brilliant old general is still replaying the cavalry charge at Balaclava and—now doddering old fool—can't see how drastically times have changed.

"Forget those tank tread things and those over-complicated motorized guns. They'll never work. Let me tell you about the heavy cavalry charge at Waterloo."

My respect for Bernie dropped cataclysmically. How could I have backed this outdated, outworn old has-been?

Worse, Kritzinger himself showed no signs of abandoning his German roots or growing Naarlen roots.

Take the annual high school theatre piece. Traditionally, the English teacher turned whatever Shakespeare text the Grade Twelves were studying into the annual school play. Kritzinger didn't believe in Shakespeare.

Someone suggested he perform a piece of Inuit theatre instead.

"No. That is cultural appropriation. Let us at choose something German," he said earnestly. "Let's do Bertold Brecht, 'The Threepenny Opera.' Translated to English."

The only other young teacher at Naarlen High, Christine Nguyen, should have supported this rebellion. Instead, she and Kritzinger argued. Christine wanted to do a punk-rock musical by a rapper I've never heard of. Kritzinger prevailed, since he was the "English" teacher. He lost the battle over the musical accompaniment to The Threepenny Opera, though. Music, stage design and costumes are the traditional purview of the arts teacher—which was Christine. She decided on a rock version of "Mack the Knife," "Pirate Jenny," etc. Rock, not jazz. With so many arguments between Christine and Kritzinger, I had grave doubts how the play would turn out.

Bernie was bombarded by comments from the women trustees, "shouldn't have hired Christine," and comments from the men of, "we knew a German English teacher wouldn't work."

I dropped by the final dress rehearsal to see how the Eberhardt vs. Christine battle of wills was shaping up.

In fact, the play looked good. The only hint of discord came when the entire cast took their bows at the end of the evening. They lined up on the front edge of the stage. Kritzinger and Christine were in the centre of the row, next to each other. Christine to the left of centre, Eberhardt to the right. Everyone to the left of Christine was hand-in-hand all the way to Christine's left hand. Everyone to the right of Eberhardt was hand in hand all the way to Eberhardt's right hand. Perhaps I was the only one to notice: the one place where the chain of hand-holding broke was between Eberhardt and Christine. The entire row put on a smile and bowed. All except one. Eberhardt merely looked serious as he bowed.

I thought, "Is he always serious like this? No, that's an unhappy face. That's a face of a man who wants to go home. Bernie's going to lose his bet with Schmidt and I'm losing Inge's new hardwood floor. Damn. Double Damn. Why the hell did Bernie have to take a bet with Schmidt? Bernie should know better. Gambling is stupid. Gambling with taxpayer money is criminal. I will never vote Bernie for mayor again. What a flawed little man. A hollowed-out shell of his former greatness."

The next day I tried to see Bernie.

"Are you paying attention to your bet, Bernie?"

"Which bet's that, mate?" he said, then ran to take a beer delivery for his pub. I wasn't reassured.

Clearly, he was not only going to lose his bet, but he was in full denial.

It didn't help when, that night at supper, Inge complained about the delay in the hardwood floor.

"Spring then, Per. No further delays, agreed?"

"Yes, my dear. Of course."

Damn. My future looked bleak.

Three nights later the school play opened. First night of two. It was a grand success, no matter whom you asked. Some raved about the music, some raved about the story, the director, the set, the costumes, the acting, the choice of play—most raved about everything. Incidentally, my neighbours, the Mafia twins, were playing guitar and double bass as part of the musical accompaniment. They and Garibaldi Senior were over the moon about the play.

Which was nice, but didn't do anything concrete for my bet on Bernie vs. Schmidt. I bumped into John Littleham.

"You were too greedy, Per. Bet too much. It's not looking good for you. You're going down big time. All the other punters are making money. Off you."

He mimicked a revolver with his right hand and pointed it at his temple.

"That's you," he said, "blowing your brains out on the stupidest bet I've ever seen."

The second performance of the school play was on a Friday night. I spent the weekend sunk in gloom. Inge would kill me come the spring if I delayed her hardwood floor yet again.

On the Monday night, I came home and found Inge talking excitedly on the phone. I heard only Inge's side of whatever it was about.

"She said what?"

"And what did he say?"

"Really?"

"Oh, that's ... beautiful."

"Yes, yes. I agree. Yes, I thought so too, right from the start."

"How perfect."

"How lovely."

"I wish I'd been a fly on the wall."

"And then what?"

"And how did you find out?"

"Who told you?"

"Who said that?"

"She did?"

I gave up trying to make sense of the half conversation I could hear. It was my turn to cook dinner anyway. When Inge was off the phone, I served supper. I could tell Inge was bursting with news.

"That was Helen Meier on the phone, Per."

"Oh, yes."

"You'll never guess, Per."

"What's that, Inge?"

"Guess."

"You said I'd never guess."

"Try."

"Umm... I give up."

"You give up, Per?"

"Yes.

"Well, Eberhardt Kritzinger and Christine Nguyen have just become engaged."

"Engaged to produce their play down south? By whom? By a theatre company down south?"

"No, Per. Do pay attention. Engaged to be married."

"Ah. At the same time. That's a coincidence. He's probably marrying that girl back in Germany. Who is Christine getting engaged to?"

"Per! I wish you would listen. They're marrying each other."

I dropped my spoon and splashed lentils all over my shirt.

"Why?"

"Because they love each other. It's so romantic. Listen. Helen won't tell me how she knows. Someone that Christine confided in spilled the beans to Helen."

"Ah. How unusual. What's the story?"

"Well, this is in confidence. You can't tell anyone, of course. Helen made me promise. What happened is the play finished Friday night. Christine and Eberhardt oversaw the clean-up, sent the kids home and then left also. Christine left a few minutes ahead of Eberhardt. You recall how on Friday the temperate fell to minus 30 with a wicked wind as well? Christine wasn't dressed for it, but since her car was in the parking lot, she knew she wouldn't be in the cold long. Then her car wouldn't start and she sat in the car getting colder and colder. Eberhardt lives a block or two from the school, so he was going to walk home and had a good jacket on. When he came out, he saw Christine shivering. The car was hopeless. It was too late for a mechanic, so he gave Christine his own jacket—so romantic, don't you think, Per—and said, 'Here. Put this on. Come with me. Two blocks to my house and then you can be warm. You must not stay here.'

"They sprinted to Eberhardt's house. It was nearing minus 40 by the time they got there—and Eberhardt—no jacket, the poor man—was shivering so violently that Christine had to take the key from him to open the door. They got inside but she was seriously worried about him. He had patches of white on his cheeks and couldn't stop shaking, all the while insisting he'd be fine soon. She found his kettle, made him a warm mug of tea with sugar for heat and a quick energy hit, made him drink that, then made him have a warm bath. After his bath she put him directly into his bed. He fell asleep almost directly. Of course, she couldn't leave with him in such a state. He still looked far too pale, and his lips had a blue tinge. She found one of his tee-shirts and tracksuit pants—she was surprised how clean and tidy everything was—she changed into those and got into the bed next to him to add her own body warmth. Very chaste, no monkey business, just ensuring he warmed up. Then she fell asleep too. The next thing she knew, it was Saturday morning and they were awake, curled up together so comfortably that neither wanted to move—just enjoying.

"Finally, he got up and made her breakfast. Pancakes, bacon and his very own home-baked bread. She says he's an amazing cook. Then they talked and talked and suddenly the day was almost done. The storm had whipped up fierce outside and being Saturday, it was again too late to call a mechanic. They made supper together. After, Christine thought Eberhardt was showing renewed signs of cold and insisted he get back under the quilts. Then she got in to warm him. But he wasn't asleep, and then apparently things were less chaste than the previous night... Oh, Per, it's such a lovely story. You'd give me your jacket if you saw me shivering outside in minus 30, wouldn't you, Per?"

"Where," I said, scraping lentils off my shirt with spoon.

Inge's tone sharpened. "Where? Why 'where?'"

"What?"

"No, why?"

"Why what?"

"Per, if you're playing stupid buggers, I'll strangle you. Why did you say 'where?' when I asked if you'd give me your jacket."

"If you were outside our house without a jacket, I'd say come inside. I wouldn't have to give you a jacket."

"That is SO stupid. But if we were drifting on an ice floe in the Beaufort Sea and I were without a jacket, would you give me yours?"

"WHAT? Being outside our house without a jacket is STUPID, but being adrift on sea ice without a jacket is NORMAL? Why would you go onto an ice floe in the ocean without a jacket? That's crazy. Unless we both were wearing dry suits, in which case I wouldn't have a jacket to give you."

She took three deep breaths, and, trying to control the rising volume in her voice said, "FORGET the ice floe. Under WHAT conditions would you give me your jacket?"

"NEVER. Nowhere."

Her volume control attempts broke down. Entirely. She always talks loudly when she's excited.

"WHAT?"

"Listen, Inge. If I promise you my jacket every time you forget yours, you'll become sloppy about remembering to bring yours. That would put us both at risk. Nei, nei. Much safer to insist you always bring yours."

"I HATE you. You're unromantic."

"Am not. And it's your turn to do the dishes."

When I got her to talk to me again, I was able to ask the important questions.

"Did Helen say whether they'll go back to Germany together?"

"Helen says they want to be able to work together. Naarlen's ideal for them. They're going to ask the school board to take them on permanently."

"What, here in Naarlen?"

"Of course, here in Naarlen, idiot."

"Will the board agree?"

"Helen says the women trustees will, and they have the majority vote. The women trustees just love what Christine did with the music and costumes for the play. And she and Eberhardt are such a cute couple. Of course, the women will give them permanent positions. And they can't wait to organize the bridal shower."

"Oh."

I went to see our mayor, that gambling fool, Bernie, at The Other Tooth the next morning.

"Seems like your risky bet against Schmidt has come out OK, Bernie. In spite of you."

"Yer, reckon I got lucky."

"Dangerous bet. Could have gone the other way, Bernie. Could have cost Naarlen Council a ton of money."

"Yer. Could have. You're right Per. Reckon I've learned my lesson. No more bets."

He hung his head. He looked again like the old cavalry officer, one whose dementia is interrupted by a brief moment of lucidity. He's just realized how ineffective mounted soldiers are against tanks and barbed wire.

He continued in subdued tones. "Lucky for me that Christine's car packed it in that night. A turning point for her and Eberhardt—them rescuing each other and then being stormbound all weekend."

"Hmm. Funny how that turned things around."

"Yer. Just like you predicted, Per, familiarity breeds. Brilliant, that. You want some coffee?"

I should have told him I don't drink with demented, reckless politicos, but seeing he'd called me brilliant, I made an effort. Maybe I could help him understand how bad gambling is. Per, the interventionist hero.

"OK."

He poured for both of us and reached under the counter for the sugar.

I stared. The ancient sugar bag was almost empty. Barely half a spoon left.

"Someone else in the bar taking sugar with coffee now, Bernie?"

"Dunno. Must have spilled some."

I stared at the ancient package. It now had black oil stains along one side. And Bernie's manner seemed evasive.

I drank my coffee. Then I left, feeling badly for Bernie. Poor fellow. Having gained the heights of mayorship of our tiny community, he was now exposed for the little man he was, scraping by on the tailcoats of Lady Luck and past glories. I would never respect him or vote for him again.

Something about him, though, nagged at me on the way home. I stopped in at Garibaldi Senior's house on the way.

"Per, how nice to see you. Is another hen loose?"

"No, no, nothing like that Francesco. Something I wanted to ask you."

"Oh, yes?"

"Did your garage do the repair work on Christine Nguyen's car after it quit on Friday night."

"Yes. I had my guys tow it into the garage. I worked on it myself. Lucky that Mr. Kritzinger rescued Christine. Could have been ugly in that storm."

"Francesco, what was wrong with her car?"

Garibaldi looked conspiratorial. "Our mayor, Mr. Halloran, is having the town council pay for the repair, and he doesn't want the details getting out. You have to promise not to tell."

"I promise."

"Somebody deliberately poured a bag of sugar into the gas tank while the car was in the school yard. Was a hell of a job to get the engine decarbonized and running again. Our mayor, such a good man, doesn't want Christine to know. Doesn't want her to think someone in Naarlen resents her. So, the council is paying the repair cost, and keeping the cause of the problem secret."

I left the Garibaldis with my head spinning.

What had Bernie said? I replayed his words silently:

"Lucky for me that Christine's car packed it in that night. A turning point for her and Eberhardt. Them rescuing each other and then being stormbound all weekend..."

and

" ... familiarity breeds..."

and

"Forget Kritzinger. It's Christine that's important."

I saw again the almost empty pack of sugar Bernie had offered me with motor oil stains down the side. There had been a matching oil stain on Bernie's sleeve.

I was struck dumb. I knew then, in a flash, who had put sugar into Christine's fuel tank. And why.

Oh, Bernie, you brilliant, scheming, tricky, underhand dog you! Who could ever doubt you, Bernie? Who could ever chalk up your victorious bet to mere luck?

It wasn't luck. It was Bernie brilliance all over again. He had set up a row of dominoes to keep Kritzinger in Naarlen, and the dominoes had tumbled one after the other just where he'd wanted them to fall. Winning the bet was a foregone conclusion. Schmidt had lost the bet the moment he proposed it. I said all along Bernie was a genius: the Isaac Newton, the Albert Einstein of politics. I always said I would vote him for mayor against any candidate in the whole damn world. And why wait until spring to give Inge her hardwood floor? She could have it immediately. I picked up my phone and dialled John Littleham.

"John, you've heard the news? Yes, it's confirmed, Eberhardt and Christine are staying in Naarlen. I'm dropping by to collect my winnings. Who said tomorrow? Not tomorrow. Right now. Expect me in five minutes. Hundred-dollar bills only, please."

The new hardwood floor was laid the very next week. Right in the middle of winter. No waiting for spring. Inge hugged me and said, "It was your surprise for me, wasn't it? Making me believe it would only be in the spring. And now, here it is. You *are* romantic, Per, in your own way. Aren't you?"

I knew that, of course, but it was nice to have Inge finally recognize it too.

Christine and Eberhardt were married in the spring. Christine's father had died when Christine was still in her teens. She asked Grampa Fergus to march her down the aisle in his stead. Fergus did. And no father could have looked prouder.

As for the bridge, ask anyone in Naarlen, for directions to the Willy Brandt Bridge and they'll stare at you blankly. The bridge—built with German taxpayer dollars—is known locally as the Harbour Bridge or as Bernie's Bridge.

*

4. The Fortune Teller

Naarlen is the Arctic. Winters are long and dark. Four months of no daylight. When, finally, the sun claws its way back above the horizon for the first time in spring, it's a time for celebration.

In years gone by the celebrations used to be famously wild. Husbands and wives cooped up together for months needed to find variety, let off steam, and feel sunshine on bare flesh. And all that was tame compared to whatever went on in the miners' dormitories on the outskirts of town.

As Naarlen grew, the imperative to set some bounds around these ever-wilder celebrations grew too. The annual Spring Fest has become a mostly tame affair in the last few years. The tradition of wearing elaborate full-face masks has ended. It led to too many surprises, divorces, paternity suits and unwanted children. The arena for celebrating the return of the sun has shifted from pubs and the infamous red-light district to the big open space behind The Church of St. Birgitta.

It's also shifted tone to a more family-orientated affair. St. Birgitta has a midnight mass, as does their competition, The Church of St. Olaf.

All this brings me to the subject of religion. I never could get it. I mean, I understand the difference between worshipping a goddess with seven arms who rides a tiger, or following the precepts of Confucius. But telling most other doctrines apart just puzzles me.

I was speaking about it with Edna in The Other Tooth recently.

I have a wary relationship with Edna, given our history. I'm even more wary when she has a beer in front of her. She has limited patience with men until her third beer. After that she likes me. By her fourth beer, she likes me a lot.

"Take the ancient Greeks and modern Christianity," I said to her. "How big is the difference between Leda being 'visited' by the swan, and Mary being 'visited' by the Holy Ghost?"

"Bugger all," said Edna. "Religious glorification of violence against women by the male patriarchy."

Edna is 6 feet four and one hundred and eighty pounds of mainly muscle. This member of the male patriarchy handles her like a grenade with a loose pin.

She continued. "Would have been a slam dunk rape case if either Leda or Mary could have been persuaded to bring charges. There was no consent, no prior relationship and damn-all material support by either father for the child's upbringing."

She was halfway through her second beer. Time for me to leave.

"Take religious headwear," she said, changing tack. "Fez, yarmulke, turban, taqiya, dastār. So many ways to express disagreement between religions. Why don't they just bury the hat shit."

"Hatchet."

"Listen Per, if I need a man to put words, or anything else, in my mouth, I'll ask."

She ordered her third beer. I left before she asked.

What gets me, though, is the sects that are 99% the same and still want to tear each other apart. It's like the cola wars. People swear by Pepsi or Coke or whatever but can't tell the difference in taste tests.

As far as I can untangle it, the bitter split between The Church of St. Birgitta and The Church of St. Olaf rests on an argument about pedobaptism. When I first heard the word, I thought it had something to do with wearing in new shoes to avoid blisters, but it turns out it's about the age at which a child should receive baptism.

There is also the question of whether churches should be decorated inside or not. The St. Birgitta folk like stained glass in glowing shades of ruby, midnight blue and gold; they like elaborate murals, frescoes, mosaics, and ornately carved altars. The St. Olaf team believes in plain white walls, clear glass windows, and unadorned wood floors and altars. The arguments are so old and deep, that the two congregations barely speak to each other.

I can only recall one incident until recently of a member switching sides. It was old Mrs. Vollman's son, Roger. He switched from St. Olaf to St. Birgitta when he turned twenty-one, because of the stained-glass windows. Mrs. V. had brought up young Roger with strict prohibition on TV and computers. Now, on days when moving clouds chase sunbeams this way and that, you'll find Roger staring mindlessly at the changing hues and intensities of the stained glass. There's a moral there, though right now it eludes me.

At the time, I asked Mrs. Vollman if Roger's switch had made her think better of the other church.

She looked at me as though I was a mouse turd in her sourdough starter.

"I wish he were dead. That way I could bury his remains and mourn him properly."

The two churches declare a truce for the Spring Fest. It is after all, held in the open space behind St. Birgitta, but the main organizers are from St. Olaf. It is also city land, an occasion for the whole town, and, as our mayor, Bernie, once explained to both congregations, they could either celebrate Spring Fest together or be locked up separately.

I might have asked Inge, my wife, what she thought about Leda and the swan vs. Mary and the Holy Ghost. The answer would have been unpredictable but interesting. Inge is a bird watcher and her first question would likely have been whether it was a trumpeter swan or a mute swan. I couldn't tell you the difference. The geese in Naarlen hiss at me aggressively when I get close. So, I don't.

Unfortunately, I couldn't ask Inge. I am the most even-tempered person in Naarlen. Ask anyone. Inge, however, is a typical Naarlander: depressed by the long darkness in winter and prone to fits of homicidal rage. Bipolar in summer, due to the never-ending daylight, the lack of sleep; in winter prone to murderous outbursts. In a temper tantrum, she'd flown south during the final month of winter to stay with an old school friend in Kirkland Lake, Ontario.

Her parting words were, "That's it. I've had it with you. I'm going to stay with Anne."

I love her dearly, of course. I mean Inge, not Anne, though Anne is nice too and I've often wondered whether ... but that's a different story... I was going to say that going south to Kirkland Lake may have been for the best until Inge regained perspective. Her unreasoning anger was triggered by two trivial events.

Firstly, she discovered that I still had not cut off the padlock that a young lady admirer had put on the harbour bridge as an expression of her crush on me.

"You said you would do it right after our anniversary lunch, Per."

"Inge, you know what happened. Sergeant Panigoniak pressganged me before I could cut the padlock. And afterwards he arrested me."

"That was six months ago and you still haven't done it. And just today, I got another card for you from that same bimbo."

"Really? What did she say?"

"Who knows? I tore it up. The only thing I know is from the envelope. She likes to decorate with butterflies and her name is Sheilagh Smith."

"But it was my card. For me. Addressed to me."

"I put it out with the trash where it belongs. Feel free to retrieve the pieces if the Sheilagh Smith and her cards mean so much to you."

"It's minus forty outside, Inge."

"Not my problem."

You can see how unreasonable the darkness was making her.

The second issue was the set of twelve wine glasses Inge's mother had given us a year back. The packaging boasted that they incorporated the latest in unbreakable, dishwasher-friendly glass technology. I broke one while washing up. Not exactly a dishwasher, but I was emulating a dishwasher by stirring everything in the sudsy sink with a long brush when the glass broke. Which did not please Inge. Apparently, the difference between eleven and twelve glasses is larger than arithmetic would have you believe.

"Don't you know anything, Per? Nobody keeps sets of eleven. Wineglasses come in fours, sixes, eights or twelves. Not eleven."

It didn't please me either. She hadn't mentioned my bleeding thumb. And who labels their glasses "unbreakable" when mere washing up can destroy them?

In the spirit of scientific enquiry, I put a wine glass into my workshop vice and applied a torque wrench to the vice. I wanted to know how much pressure would break the wine glass. The answer was "surprisingly little."

Inge heard the glass breaking and came running.

"What are you thinking of, Per! Wasn't breaking one enough?"

"I took proper precautions, Inge. Look—protective gloves and eyewear. No cuts at all this time."

"Damn your protective wear. What about my wine glasses?"

"You said no one keeps sets of eleven. You said a set of eight is acceptable. Which allows me to test two more. In case there is a variability in the results."

It was about then that the Seasonal Affectivness Disorder got to her. Prolonged lack of sunlight and critically low levels of vitamin D.

"That's it. I've had it with you," she shouted and went to pack her bags for Kirkland Lake.

It turned my mind back to religion—you'll see why in a minute. In particular, couldn't the priests at St. Olaf and St. Birgitta find better subjects to argue over than stained glass vs. not stained glass? Shouldn't they be debating whether true evil exists? Is the devil real? And if he or she is real, had he/she taken possession of Olga or was Olga merely a lonely soul crying out in torment? I'll come to Olga in a minute. Bear with me.

I was saying Inge's departure is how I came to be on my own during the Naarlen Spring Fest. Spring is, of course, the time when a young man's fancy turns to the pleasures his mate can bring. Only my mate wasn't there. She was in Kirkland Lake with Anne (who might also bring pleasures of spring, but was equally not there).

I wandered the grounds of the Naarlen Spring Fair feeling low. I tried my hand at throwing darts for prizes, shooting at the cardboard seals for prizes, fishing with magnets for prizes, and buying cotton candy. I watched Edna win the boulder-carrying competition. None of it cheered me up. Then I came to the tent where Olga was doing duty as Madam X, the fortune teller.

Olga was a long-time friend or ours. Her husband, Jorge, had died of a sudden heart attack a year previously and we'd seen nothing of them since then. I mean obviously we hadn't seen Jorge since—that would be downright weird—but I'm trying to say we'd seen nothing of Olga either. She'd taken the reins of his fishing fleet, sold it for a handsome profit then taken off on a trip down south. I'd heard word that she'd spent time in a health spa down south, gone hiking in the Himalayas and returned looking trim and fit. None of that prepared me for how gorgeous she was looking. The Madam X costume with a mysterious veil and lots of flimsy gauze merely added to that allure.

Olga stood as I entered and gave me her hand.

"Per. How nice."

"Olga, you're looking ... wonderful."

She held onto my hand longer than was strictly necessary. Her palm was warm and soft. At length she gave my hand a final squeeze said, "Sit. We'll catch up as Per and Olga, soon. But now, Madam X must foretell your future. You will drink tea with me, and I will foretell all."

My knees buckled. I sat. I could feel the afterglow warmth of where her hand had rested on mine.

We were still staring at each other.

"It's so hot in this tent," she said, and opened two top buttons on her blouse.

She put a crystal ball on the desk between us and began.

"Your future is obscured—as though behind a gauze veil."

The only gauze I could see was her blouse. She leaned forward. The gauze strained to obscure, but wasn't up to the task. I saw why Jorge had a heart attack. I might have one any moment too. She was magnificent.

She picked up a tea bag in each hand, and dangled the bags by their strings. The bags swung hypnotically across her ample chest, just at the critical height. I shifted my angle of view to see past them.

Perhaps she sensed what I was gazing at. Without any embarrassment she said, “They’re all natural.”

“Really?”

“So many aren’t these days, Per, you have no idea.”

“Nei, nei, I wouldn’t know. I’ve been married for many years.”

“Which one would you like, Per?”

“Pardon?”

“Right or left, Per?”

They looked the same to me. Both wonderful.

I mumbled, “I’m married.”

I’m not sure if she heard. She didn’t acknowledge it. Merely said, “One is Lapsang Souchong, the other is Darjeeling.”

I was astounded. “You have named them? I never knew a woman to name her...” I trailed off. She wasn’t embarrassed, but I felt myself blushing.

“Well, not me, Per. Other people named them.”

“Which other people?”

“People who appreciate them, Per.”

She leaned even further, the gauze blouse gave up another layer of obfuscation under the pressure from within. The demarcation between pale skin and dark centres became even clearer. There was a hint of pink just where...

I got up shakily, “I need air.”

I stumbled out of the tent.

My brain was pounding and my heart was a puddle of molten lead. Or was it the other way around? I needed to cool off. Water!

I staggered up to the Church of St. Birgitta. It was the only place I could think of. It was also the nearest building. The gloom inside temporarily blinded me. I paused and then—miracle of miracles—I saw what I needed. The baptismal font. St. Birgitta be praised, it was filled with water. I stuck my head in. I stayed under as long as I could, then emerged feeling marginally in control of myself again.

It didn't last. Father René Guillaume frightened the bejabbers out of me. Black cassock in the dark, I hadn't seen him until he spoke.

"Per."

"Jesus H. Christ on a Montréal bagel, and hold the mustard! You nearly gave me a heart attack."

When my heart restarted, I thought, "Now he'll give me heck me for sticking my head in the holy water, or for blaspheming."

He didn't. He just stared at me. I must have been a sight. Hair plastered to my head. Water streaming off me.

We stared silently. As my eyes adjusted to the gloom, I noticed an oddity.

His hair was also sopping wet. He was standing in an even larger puddle than I was. His shirt was near transparent, it was so wet.

We both spoke. At the same time, same words.

"You've been talking to *OLGA*."

"*YOU'VE* been talking to Olga."

After another silence, he said, "She's possessed by the devil. I know the signs. I've seen this before. I am going now to do the exorcism."

He pointed to his paraphernalia. A bible, a censer, incense already lit and smoking, a bell, a cross and various other bits and bobs.

"Listen, René," I said. "You're a priest. Sworn to celibacy. You know nothing of women. Sure, they may all seem like devils on a bad day, and some of them even seem like devils on a good day. I'm a married man, I know. I assure you, though, Olga's no devil, nor possessed. She's a lonely soul crying out for human contact. Her husband of many years is dead. She's all alone without a soulmate. Now that I'm thinking straight again, I'm going back to do the right thing. To offer her decent human solace. One caring human for another. Reaching out to touch and comfort."

"No," he said. "I forbid it. The danger is too great. The devil in her has already warped your judgment. I may not be a married man, but I am a theologian. I know evil. I recognize the devil. He exists, evil exists and I can smell both. In Olga."

"You forbid it, René? No. I forbid you. I'm blocking the doorway. See? You will not get past me."

"Come, Per. We're both reasonable men. Violence is no answer. Except when dealing with the devil."

"You are prepared to use violence against Olga?"

"No more than needed, Per."

"You shall not."

"What if, Per, I could show you some evidence that might change your mind? Are you open-minded enough to view the evidence?"

"Where is this idiotic evidence?"

"In the sacristy."

"The what?"

"A small room on the side of the church. You can see the door. There."

"Very well. Show me."

We walked over to the door. He unlocked it and stood aside. I walked in.

"The light switch is over the desk," he said. "Would you mind turning it on."

I walked to his desk and looked for the switch. Behind me the door closed. There was no switch. I heard him relock the door, from outside.

"Open up, René!"

"It's for your own good, Per. I'll let you out after the exorcism."

I heard him leave. It took me an hour to figure out how to climb out of the one high window without breaking my neck. By then it was dark and the fairground was deserted. Madam X's tent was closed.

I went home to look for a phone number for Olga. To check if she was OK. Inge was standing in the entrance hall of our house with her bags. She gave me a huge hug.

"Per, I missed you."

"I missed you too. You have no idea. How was Kirkland Lake? And Anne?"

"Very nice, but she became tedious after a few weeks. I'm happy to be back."

"I'm happy to have you back."

Neither of us wanted the hug to end, and what with one thing and another, it didn't seem like the right time to ask for Olga's phone number.

I think it was a week later that Inge broke the news to me. We were having dinner.

"Have you heard the big scandal at St. Birgitta?"

"No, what scandal, Inge?"

"René Guillaume."

"Oh, no. What did he do?"

My heart sank. Was René charged with Olga's murder? I feared the worst. And I had done nothing to check on Olga. I felt sick.

"René left St. Birgitta, Per."

"Huh. Fired no doubt. Or arrested?"

"Not at all, Per, he resigned."

"Why?"

"He's become priest at St. Olaf's."

"What! No one switches sides like that. Except Roger, and he doesn't count. Why? And what happened to Father Mulcahey at St. Olaf?"

"Mulcahey fell off his bicycle and is recuperating down south with a hairline fracture in his leg."

"And why did René leave St. Birgitta?"

"An issue of doctrine. René decided that St. Birgitta's doctrine is flawed and St. Olaf's is correct. You can imagine how both congregations are buzzing at this."

"Which doctrine, Inge? The pedobaptism? The decorations in the church?"

"No, silly. Those are trivial. He left because of the big elephant-in-the-room issue."

"What elephant, Inge?"

"Oh, Per. Sometimes you're so innocent. Priests at St. Birgitta are celibate. Barely any contact with women. Priests at St. Olaf are encouraged to marry and have families. It's a huge doctrinal difference. Didn't you know?"

My mouth hung open. I hadn't known.

"Inge?"

"Yes, dear?"

"Why now?"

"What?"

"Why did René decide *NOW* that the doctrinal difference mattered?"

"Ah, Per. That is the juicy part of what I wanted to tell you. Word is that René is courting Olga. Did you know she's back from her travels and looking absolutely fabulous?"

"Ja, ja. Nei, nei. I mean, yes, I knew she was back. No, I didn't know about fabulous."

"We'll have to have them both over for dinner soon."

"Ja, ja, of course, whatever."

In the event, it was Olga who invited Inge and me first, for a dinner.

The day before the dinner date, René tracked me down and took me aside. He looked embarrassed.

"Per, when you and Inge come for supper tomorrow, I'm invited too, you won't mention how I thought Olga was the devil, will you? It was very silly, very wrong, and I want to put it behind me."

I considered. Given that Inge might misinterpret my motives in this whole saga if the details became known, I thought it best to agree. I mimed zipping my lips.

René breathed deeply. "Thank you, Per. You've no idea how much that means. Olga and I are not yet... you know, it's very early in getting to know each other. These early stages are delicate so... We're not ... although I hope... You're a good, kind, generous person. I will say an extra prayer for you every night this week."

Dinner was interesting. Olga looked stunning. And René was like a man under a spell. Olga treated him politely but just like another dinner guest, not a boyfriend. I amused myself by thinking, well, if a devil—hypothetically—had possession of Olga, a great way to wreak havoc on both St. Birgitta and St. Olaf was precisely by leading René on just enough to make him switch loyalties at church. I chuckled inwardly at this notion.

After dinner Olga said, "Inge, something to drink? Tisane? Coffee? Tea? Or something stronger?"

"Tea please, Olga."

Olga held up two bundles of tea bags.

"This is all I have in the house. Left over from the Spring Fair. Per came. I offered him the same choice."

She raised the bags in her left hand for emphasis, "Darjeeling," then raised the other hand for emphasis. "Lapsang souchong. All natural. No herbicides."

"Darjeeling please, Olga," said Inge. "What did Per have? He doesn't often drink tea."

"Per reminds me of how Jorge was. You know men, after a few years of marriage, they need to consult their wives over every decision. Per couldn't make up his minds. Poor dear. He even tried to excuse his indecision by saying he was married. So sweet, really."

I watched in turmoil. Had I misinterpreted everything in that damn fortune-telling tent? Had I nearly made a colossal, irrecoverable blunder? Had Olga's every action been totally innocent?

It seemed so. I damned myself for an idiot.

Until time came to leave.

It was when we were saying our goodbyes. Inge had her back turned to hug and chat with René. Olga used the opportunity to give me a hug that she turned into something far more than a friendly dinner farewell. Her face was so close to mine that only she heard when I gasped, "You *ARE* the devil, aren't you?"

She wasn't put off. She hugged a moment longer, then stepped back and gave me a lazy smile and a very private wink.

Then she leaned close one more time and said, "Shh. Our secret. And I have to finish unveiling your ... future ... for you. You'd like to see your futures unveiled, wouldn't you, Per? Meet me down at the old fishing harbour Wednesday morning 10 a.m. Alone."

I needed another baptismal font. Urgently. There wasn't one.

I drove Inge and myself home. I had difficulty keeping the car in its lane, or even on the road. Inge chattered heedlessly. "Such a lovely dinner," she said. "I'm so glad Renée took the initiative to leave St. Birgitta, although they don't seem like a couple. Maybe with time. We'll have to return the dinner invitation for Olga soon. That'll be fun, right, Per?"

I didn't know whether to groan, laugh, cry, drool or gibber like a demented monkey in a banana factory.

"Per?"

"Yes, dear," I said finally, and tried to concentrate on the driving.

The old fishing harbour wouldn't be most people's first choice for an amorous meeting place, but Olga had owned a fishing fleet. She knew all the secret hiding places. I had no doubt what would follow—although, as it turned out I was wrong.

On Wednesday morning, I arrived early and as giddy as a teenager on a first date.

I stood on the edge of the old wharf, watching the fish finning in and out of the wharf supports while I waited. Olga must have been in a state of eager anticipation too. She arrived early. Whatever her inner frame of mind, outwardly she was cool, composed and as beautiful as ever. More so, even. She'd dressed with care: a blue scarf, a matching blue jersey, open to reveal a crisp white cotton shirt, top button undone; skirt and leather boots up to just below the knees—a nice touch to accentuate her lovely long legs.

She walked up to me and took both my hands in hers. We were gazing into each other's eyes silently—one of those precious moments when a smile and the pressure of the hand will communicate more than any words. Our silent communion was interrupted by a voice, a shrill, angry voice. The kind of voice you'd have if you'd been trying to get through to customer service at Naarlen Telecom or Naarlen Airlines.

"Mr. Pederson."

I looked. It was a scruffily dressed young woman. My first impression was that her hair could do with a wash, and probably the rest of her could too. Dangling next to her greasy hair were crudely homemade butterfly earrings.

"Ja?" I said.

"My name is Sheilagh Smith," said the angry woman.

"Ja?" I said.

"Don't you know me?"

"Nei, never heard of you."

"You should have. I've been sending you a card a week for over a year. Which you never answered. Not once."

She launched into a run at Olga and me. It wasn't a good or particularly fast run, but Olga and I were taken unawares. I managed to partially sidestep before she caught me a glancing blow and ricocheted into Olga. Olga went into the water. Arctic water. No ice at this time of year, but still lethally cold. As close to freezing point as makes no difference. I spun around toward the water to see how Olga was doing. She had surfaced and was facing me, her eyes on me, but wide in icy shock.

I was opening my mouth to yell, "Just hold on, I'm phoning for help," when a hard push on the small of my back sent me toppling too. Sheilagh Smith again.

It's funny how time slows down in moments like that and how trivial things stick in your mind:

Olga's expression told me that, with her angle of view, she hadn't seen Sheilagh push me. I could tell even in that split second that Olga thought I was jumping in to rescue her. The second thing I focused on was how beautifully the cold water was shaping her white cotton shirt. I wanted to remember it, to become a sculptor and make a thousand versions in white marble.

All that was crystal clear to me as I tumbled to possible death by hypothermia.

Then the shock of the cold hit me and all slow-motion analysis went out of the window.

"Oof."

That first gasp—an explosive inhalation—is dangerous. It's an involuntary reaction to the extreme temperature change. But if your mouth is underwater that inhalation will kill you. I was lucky. The force of my fall had pushed the water up on either side of me but dug a space around my head. It must have been the same for Olga.

If your heart isn't stopped by the shock, and you can get ashore to warmth quickly you may survive. You have minutes only.

I wasn't thinking about that. I was reacting. Primally. I panicked and thrashed toward Olga. She had reached the wooden support pilings and was slowly, painfully, clawing her way up an old wooden ladder. I hung on below. Neither of us had enough strength to climb all the way up. Our bodies had already shut down blood flow to our arms and legs—

all to preserve core body temperature. Fortunately, we had been seen. Fishermen and dockworkers came running, secured us before we fell back, roped us and hauled us into waiting ambulances.

Both Olga and I overnighted in hospital, although we were in separate wards and didn't see each other. In the morning I had one last check before discharge, with a psychologist of all things. A kindly old fellow by the name of Paul Allen. He sat with both Inge and me.

"I need you both to understand," he said, "that Per will have some odd reactions to life in the coming weeks, perhaps even longer. That's normal. He will have at least some form of PTSD. It may take many forms. For instance, intense inexplicable emotions such as an unreasoning hatred for Ms. Olga Harkonnen, whom he so bravely tried to save. Hatred, because part of his brain will blame her for the risk he had to take."

"Nei, nei, never," I said. "Olga's a dear friend, a delightful person."

"She for her part may feel strong and illogical emotions for you, Per, if she associates you with her PTSD."

"Surely, not bad emotions," I said fondly.

"Sometimes yes, sometimes no. It's not a matter of logic," he said. "In fact," he said, "Ms. Harkonnen has asked me to share with you that she's aware of your very gallant dive into the water to save her ... "

"Is she really?' I said, and found I had to wipe my eyes repeatedly. "Paul, Inge, would you mind giving me a minute alone? I'm a little overwhelmed by her kind words."

They handed me a paper tissue for my eyes and stepped outside.

After a decent interval, they knocked and re-entered.

Paul handed me another paper tissue.

I wiped and he continued, "As I was saying. Emotions will well up uncontrollably at the oddest of times. Which is why we prefer to have spouses present for these interviews. So. Where was I? Oh, Yes. Ms. Olga Harkonnen has asked me to share with you that although she's aware of your heroic dive into the water to save her, and she understands why Mayor Halloran has proposed a bravery medal for you, she never wants to see you again. It's association, of course, with a trauma and not necessarily a reflection on you. However, she also says that any man who attracts such unhinged assailants must have something deeply wrong with him."

"*Jævlig fittetryne*. Olga Harkonnen is a stupid, idiotic, thankless, brainless witch. A deeply ugly person. If I never see her again, it will be too soon. Please tell her from me."

"A totally normal reaction," said Paul calmly. I'll be sure to let her know. I've noted down the exact words. I believe it's a helpful catharsis for both parties not to bottle this up or sugarcoat. Please, if you meant bitch, don't say witch.'

"I meant bitch."

"Thank you, I have noted the correction. Anything else I should tell her, Per?"

I added some phrases that I don't need to repeat here.

"And, Paul, let's be clear." I said, "The unhinged assailant is Inge's fault. Inge tore up her letters."

"No, no, Per," said Inge. "You encouraged the young woman by not cutting the padlock off the bridge months ago. I reminded you repeatedly."

"Now, now," said Paul. "I do couples counselling, but what with Naarlen's unique problem of sunlight imbalance, you'd have to get on the waiting list for next year. In the meantime, go home and enjoy your lives. Try not to kill each other."

We left, trudging home. I wondered whether Inge would question why I happened to be with Olga at the fishing harbour. Instead, Inge slipped her hand into mine.

"I'm proud of you, Per. A medal for bravery. You're such a good man. What would we Naarlanders do without you?"

My mood brightened. She was right, she always is, of course. Naarlanders depend on me. I'm the Superman and Batman of Naarlen rolled into one. Possibly the only sane person in this island of rogues and crackpots.

I squeezed Inge's hand and we walked happily home.

*

5. Attila The Cat

Naarlen is seventy-eight degrees north. That's the Arctic, so you might expect some strange things here. In my opinion though, life here is even stranger than you'd expect.

Consider the problem of cherry pie. It's my experience that life either hands you an uncooked cherry pie with no oven to cook it in, or an oven with no pie. Or it hands you one and takes back the other. But occasionally, just occasionally, it offers you both. When that happens, you'd better grab quickly.

Take the case of Inge wanting a cat. The urge came on her suddenly. I love my wife, but a cat?

"Why not, Per?"

"Do you know even one man who is a cat person, Inge?"

"I'm sure they exist."

"It's a woman thing, Inge. Women start with one cat, pretty soon they have thirteen. The cats shred the furniture, the carpets and the drapes. The house smells, the cats have kittens, and soon there are fifty-two cats and half of them are pregnant again."

"That is SO ridiculous, Per."

It was a debate that wouldn't go away.

Around the same time, Klaas van Vuuren, the owner-editor of the Naarlen Herald ("Our Community's Voice in the Arctic") offered me a part-time gig on his newspaper.

Klaas and I know each other from the odd poker game. He's a straight shooter. Plays well, plays honestly and pays up on time, unlike some. A decent, honourable man. I like the old duffer.

Now Inge wanting a cat, and Klaas wanting me to write for his rag, might not sound like the cherry pie and oven, but it is. Bear with me and you'll see it too.

"Why me, Klaas? I'm no journalist."

"Trudie Lanscomb, who writes our 'Dear Aunt Maude' column, is on leave for a few weeks. She suggested you'd be fabulous. I think so too. It's something you can do over a spare hour at lunch or in the evenings. It doesn't take much time."

"Trudie is Aunt Maude?"

“Never, never, never reveal that. Please, Per. It’s a BIG secret.”

“Fine, but Trudie suggested me to stand in for her? For your etiquette and lonely-hearts column?”

“Tja, she said that you’re the ideal Aunt Maude. You’d still write under the name ‘Aunt Maude.’ Trudie’s been gone a week and this is pressing.”

“Klaas, is this a paying job?”

“Free beer at The Other Tooth. Mondays to Thursdays.”

“And Fridays?”

“Free urinal.”

“Nei, nei. I don’t drink beer and the urinal stinks.”

I was ready to turn him down, except ... the cherry pie and oven.

We haggled a bit, agreed a real salary, and I became the new Aunt Maude for the week. Starting Tuesday and ending Friday.

“So, Klaas, where is Trudie?”

“She’s been dating some guy on the Internet, somewhere in Africa, and they’ve become serious, engaged even, can you believe? She’s gone to Africa to meet him in the flesh. First time meeting. If all goes well, they’ll marry.”

“All in Africa?”

“Tja, tja, Africa. Ethiopia or Kenya or some such. I don’t recall. She’ll come back here after, either still single or with a new husband. Don’t worry you’re only filling in until the end of the week when she’s due back. Secret, remember? Can’t tell readers that Aunt Maude has changed.”

“Fine, I won’t even tell Inge. This guy in Africa, though, is he for real?”

Klaas shrugged. "Tja, tja, if Aunt Maude, the queen of lonely-hearts advice says he's legit, then he's legit."

I showed up at the Herald on Tuesday morning. The offices were noisy because of renovations one floor up. Klaas had to shout to make himself heard.

"This is your desk and computer, Per. All email comes to you. If it's a bill or a payment, print a paper copy for my desk. I don't do email. Otherwise, it's for Aunt Maude. My desk is there..."

He pointed to a desk twenty feet away from mine.

"Ah."

"Three more weeks, Per, and we'll be one of the oldest continuously published newspapers in North America."

"Really, Klaas, that's amazing."

"Oh, yes. We started when Naarlen was still a German colony. Back then the paper published in German and was called 'Der Klein-Berlinicher Berichter.'"

"Catchy."

"So, Per, you can imagine, the next three weeks are SO exciting. To get the paper into the record books."

"Three more weeks, Klaas?"

"Nineteen days exactly. I can't tell you how proud I will be when we break that record. It's my life's work. I'll die happy. I can barely sleep. Anyway, I'll let you get to it."

The first letter for Aunt Maude came from "Concerned Mother." I couldn't make head or tail of it.

Dear Aunt Maude,

I'm worried about my daughter and the things they teach young girls in school.

Today she came home and said they had to learn about the periodic table. She's only ten and nowhere near puberty. Plus, it's a co-ed class, and the teacher is male. I am outraged. This is a sensitive topic and should not be taught in a room with boys. When girls are old enough, they should be taught by a woman teacher in a girls-only class.

I have written a strongly worded letter to Principal Lundgren about this, but have received no reply.

I'm hoping to draw support from other women who read your column. I believe it's time in Naarlen for an organization of mothers to address this shocking way of teaching our daughters. I'd be willing to chair it, and propose to call it "Mothers Against the Periodic Table." Please, Aunt Maude, invite all other concerned mothers to contact me through your column.

Concerned Mother.

(Name withheld at the writer's request)

I looked at back issues of Aunt Maude's column and saw Aunt Maude's style. The advice usually took the form of "Yes, blah blah," or "Yes, but, blah blah," and Aunt Maude always referred to herself in the third person.

That seemed straight forward. I typed up my reply under her letter on the typesetting app.

Dear Concerned Mother,

You're quite right to turn to Aunt Maude. Lundgren is a useless waste of space. You'll never get results from him. I know people who've waited more than a year for that deadbeat to settle his poker debts.

You're also quite right to keep an eye on what he's teaching your daughter.

I encourage other mothers to contact "Concerned Mother" directly: Mrs. Jean Fantucci, 23 High River Street, Naarlen Centre. Phone: 867-21-21.

Best of luck,
Aunt Maude.

There was also a letter for Aunt Maude from Iqbal Srinivasan. Iqbal has tried for years to get elected as mayor of Naarlen. He doesn't stand a chance against Bernie Halloran, so Iqbal's views of Bernie are clouded by years of resentment. I considered how to answer Iqbal's letter and finally entered the following into the typesetting app:

Dear Aunt Maude,

Don't your readers find it shameful that our mayor, Bernard Halloran, engages in false advertising at his public house, The Other Tooth? He encourages the weak-minded to drink with *false promises that the beer is free. Only, afterwards drinkers discover it's $30 to use the urinals. And the urinal fees are not on the menu.*

Shame on Bernard Halloran. Doesn't Naarlen deserve better from its mayor?

Sincerely,

Iqbal Srinivasan.

Naarlen City Councillor.

Dear Iqbal,

Aunt Maude has no opinion on the social utility of a public house happy hour. However, Aunt Maude does believe in competition to ensure fairer prices for consumers.

If one wished to compete with Mr. Halloran, one could park a truck trailer carrying several pay-per-use portable toilets on the street opposite Mr. Halloran's public house, and undercut Mr. Halloran's urinal charges.

Sincerely,

Aunt Maude.

On Wednesday morning Klaas said to me, "You've got mail coming in like I've never seen. We sold out all our copies and had to do another print run."

"Did you read my column, Klaas?"

"Good job whatever you're doing, but I never read Aunt Maude. I have to worry how to keep the business side running and it's hard."

"Maybe I can advise you, Klaas. I know more about accounting than agony columns."

I scooped some bills off his desk and shuffled through them.

"Here's a big one, Klaas. What's this for?"

"Liability insurance for the coming year."

"Oof. It's not cheap."

"No."

"How long has the paper been around?"

"One hundred and ninety-nine years. I told you, the big two hundred is coming."

"How often have you been sued in all that time?"

"Never, Per. We're a community paper. People in Naarlen play nicely with each other. People here are not mean, and we don't sue each other."

"Then let me save you a lot of money, Klaas. Cancel your liability insurance. You don't need it."

He stared at me thoughtfully, then nodded.

"You're right. We've been paying this useless stuff for almost 200 years. I'll cancel immediately."

I went back to Aunt Maude's desk and opened the typesetter app for the coming edition. I copied in letters replying to "Concerned Mother" from a bunch of my fellow Norwegians.

They called Lundgren "*et svensk drittsekk*" (a Swedish shitbag) and "*svensk drittsekk med sitt gule og blå.*"

I left "*svensk drittsekk*" untranslated. Aunt Maude does not allow vulgar English in her column. But Norwegian vulgarity about Swedes was probably OK. It's more a cultural thing than true vulgarity. In any case, what do we reporters say?

"The public has a right to know."

Lundgren himself, had the cheek to send in a letter explaining something or other. It was long and boring. I put it into the trash unread. Who wants to read letters from a *drittsekk*?

There were many replies about Mothers Against the Periodic Table. I published a sampling. My favourite proposed additional societies: *Mothers for the Conservation of Momentum*, and *Mothers Against the Repeal of Newton's Third Law.*

I also created and typeset my own letter to Aunt Maude from a fake persona I invented called "Cat Husband."

Dear Aunt Maude,

My wife got a cat two years ago, and two more last year. All are pregnant for the second time and we now have 18 cats with more on the way. Should I be concerned?

Sincerely,

Cat Husband.

My reply, as Aunt Maude, was:

Dear Cat Husband,

Aunt Maude believes you have every reason to be concerned. For many people, women particularly, cats are an addiction similar to crack cocaine. Having tried just one, perhaps at a dinner party or friend's house, the addicts crave ever higher doses. Speedy counselling for your wife is a must if the cats are not to empty your bank account, destroy your home, your career, your marriage and your social life.

Aunt Maude is curious to know how many men readers, and how many women readers would allow even one cat in their home. Aunt Maude invites all readers to send in their answer. Remember to identify your sex. We will publish the poll result shortly.

Thank you,

Aunt Maude (Yay, dogs!)

You see now why I say life had handed me both a cherry pie and the oven in which to cook it. I would leave a copy of the Herald in every room of our house until Inge had read this truly horrifying tale.

There was also a Nigerian phishing email. As usual, it purported to come from a family member or friend or coworker who claimed to need money urgently.

"Klaas," I shouted across to his desk, "is Trudie in Lagos?"

"Where?"

The workmen were drilling again upstairs, and Klaas's hearing is not great at the best of times. I shouted more loudly. "Lagos."

"Laos?"

"Lagos."

"No," he shouted back. "That's in Vietnam. I told you, Trudie's in Africa. Kenya, Ethiopia, Nigeria or some such."

Instead of trashing the email, I published it. A Naarlen public service.

Dear Readers,

Aunt Maude reminds Herald readers of the danger of sending money or bank information in reply to phishing emails. Here is a classic example. Someone is claiming to be Naarlen's own Trudie Lanscomb and in desperate need of money.

Trudie is indeed away from Naarlen, but is not in Lagos, and why would she turn to Klaas van Vuuren for help instead of the Canadian embassy? None the less, it would be easy for any open-hearted Naarlander to be fooled by such an email appeal. Aunt Maude reprints the email here as a warning that scam email reaches everywhere, even Naarlen. The scam email follows below my signature.

Your ever-vigilant,

Aunt Maude.

Dear Klaas,

I'm in desperate straits. The man that lured me to Lagos has absconded with my passport, my airline ticket and money. The hotel I'm in will kick me onto the streets at the end of the week. Please wire money urgently.

Desperate.

Trudie Lanscomb.

That evening at dinner, Inge was furious.

"I was at the hairdresser today. You can't believe the anger there about the latest Aunt Maude column.

The whole salon, we are all writing to Maude in protest."

I was puzzled. "Is it about the Vietnamese spammer?"

"No. It's about the cats."

I'd been so preoccupied I'd almost forgotten about the cats. My oven and cherry pie.

On Thursday, Aunt Maude received a letter from a man asking for dating advice. Those of you who followed my debacle with Olga will know that romance is not my strong suit.

I went to that single woman, par-excellence, Edna to ask her advice. Approaching Edna requires careful timing. She dislikes men before her first beer, and likes them in dangerous ways after her third. I timed my approach carefully. I didn't understand a word of her advice. My Norwegian background makes some English idioms impenetrable, but I wrote down Edna's words faithfully. I published them, together with the miner's question.

> *Dear Aunt Maude,*
>
> *I'm a mining engineer at Naarlen Palladium. I have a good job and good education. I'm tall, broad-shouldered, and people tell me I'm good looking. I'm fit and health conscious, especially about what I eat. However, I never know how to start conversations with women I see in bars and such. What is a good opening line?*
>
> *Yours, Tongue-Tied.*

Dear Tongue-Tied,

Aunt Maude has it on good authority that if you were in a bar one night, say, sitting next to a woman with whom you wanted to strike up a conversation, the following would be a good opening strategy:

Lean over to the woman and whisper quietly into her ear, "If I am what I eat, I could be you by the morning."

Do let Aunt Maude and her gentle readers know how it works out for you.

Best of luck,

Aunt Maude.

The same day I received a follow-on from the Vietnamese fraudster. Again, I published it, with another warning to readers.

Gentle Readers,

You may be surprised to hear how persistent and ingenious the phishing emails are. The scamsters obviously read Aunt Maude's warning yesterday, including the part about the Canadian Embassy. Their cheeky message follows my signature.

Stay alert, stay safe,

Aunt Maude.

Klaas,

The Canadian Consulate has thrown me out. They claim there is no such place as Naarlen. Send money. Or send me your bank account info for transfer. Urgent.

Trudie Lanscomb.

Feeling pleased with my day's work, I ambled over to Klaas's desk. He was again looking frazzled.

"Bills, bills, Per. Nothing but bills."

"Here," I said. "Let me have a look. Oh, another big one. What's this?"

"Property insurance."

"Have you ever made a claim, Klaas?"

"Once. Forty years ago. When I started work here. A kettle shorted out some electrical wiring."

"Do you remember the repair bill?"

"Tja, Per, about fifty dollars. A lot of money back then. And the electric outlet still can't take a kettle. There's a notice stuck on the outlet."

I wondered how much use that notice would be. He had pasted notices on plugs, switches and locks everywhere.

"Reverse fan direction in summer."

"Wash hands after using washroom."

"Do not store printer paper here."

"Fridge is cleaned out every Friday."

"Leave this light on at night."

"Keep this door closed at all time."

"Hang spare key here."

"This is Klaas's stapler. Do not borrow."

Who could ever read all that nonsense? But back to his insurance bill.

“And by how much, Klaas, did the insurance premium increase after you claimed on the electric repair.”

He looked embarrassed. “About fifty dollars more than the previous year.”

“Huh. Klaas, do yourself a favour, cancel your property insurance. Go buy your wife something nice.”

“Oh... I’m not married you know... I sometimes wondered whether... Trudie and I ... but then this thing with the man in Africa ... she’s genuinely fond of me ... once she hinted... I’ll have to see ... maybe Africa won’t work out ... and then I could ... if she would...

I couldn’t stand around all day listening to this drivel. I cut him short.

“Buy yourself something then. Cancel the property insurance now.”

I waited until I was sure he’d picked up the phone to the insurance people, then I left. Honestly, some people need a nursemaid standing over them.

That was also the day the replies to my cat poll came flooding in. I thought I’d have to make up a few scare letters to get my point across to Inge, but there were plenty of genuine letters to make the point. Most came from disgruntled husbands and ex-husbands blaming a cat for marital estrangement. I published those letters with glee.

That night, for the first time in days, Inge was silent on the subject of wanting a cat. I sensed my campaign was changing her mind.

By the fourth day, Friday, my gig was relatively routine. There was yet another email from the Vietnamese scammers. It followed the usual pattern.

Klaas,

I know you were angry with my decision to go to Africa. I admit it was a huge mistake on my part. But I learned from it. I learned where my heart truly lies. Please, dear, dear Klaas, bring me home. Send the airfare. Please.

Your loving Trudie.

A typical play on the mark's emotions. I deleted the email, and blacklisted the sender to block future emails.

I took care of a few other emails, then walked over to The Other Tooth to have a coffee with Bernie.

I never got that coffee. There was an ambulance and two police cars outside The Other Tooth. The ambulance men were loading a big, groaning fellow onto a stretcher. The police cars were loading an angry Edna.

My friend, Sergeant David Panigoniak, was supervising.

"Ai, David."

"Ai, Per, qaniungi?"

"Good, thank you, David. What happened here?"

"See the big guy on the stretcher?"

"Ja."

"He's an engineer from over at the palladium mines. He was sitting next to Edna in the bar, and tried to strike up a conversation. He whispered something in her ear, then she decked him."

"Must have been before her first beer, but what on earth did he say?"

David looked embarrassed. He opened his notebook, stared at it, then shut his book again.

"I won't repeat it."

It didn't matter. I'd figured out what he'd said to Edna. I left before she caught sight of me.

I walked back to the Herald offices feeling restless. There was an email from the mining engineer and one from Lundgren, both threatening to sue the newspaper. I deleted the messages. No need to bother Klaas until they got their lawyers involved. I carried the kettle into the kitchen, got some coffee and a mug from the kitchen cupboard and waited for the kettle to boil.

Klaas walked into the office and went to his desk. I walked over. "Anything new today, Klaas?"

"You mean other than only sixteen sleeps left for me to break the record? You don't know what this means to me, Per."

"Two hundred years. I understand why you're excited."

"Actually, there is something Per. There's been a traffic accident near The Other Tooth. I know you're not a reporter, but would you mind checking it out for us?"

"Sure. It's a slow day on the Aunt Maude beat."

I ambled back to The Other Tooth. Suffering Jaysus. Talk about chaos. I'd forgotten it was happy hour at The Other Tooth. Which would make it busy enough. But now police cars with flashing lights were blocking off the road outside the pub. I looked past the police cars. Some idiot had parked a truck trailer opposite the pub. A second truck, a beer delivery truck, had backed out from The Other Tooth's loading area, backed into the parked trailer and knocked it over. The trailer's load lay on the ground next to the upended trailer: three portable toilets, lying on their sides. One of them had someone inside, trying to climb out while the bystanders stood well back.

It was like watching Count Dracula emerge from his coffin: fascinating, but you wouldn't want to get close enough to offer him a hand.

Two police constables stood near me watching the figure emerge.

"Shit," said the first constable.

"Ah-huh," agreed the second.

Councillor Iqbal Srinivasan was shouting furiously at the constables, "Help him! Help him!"

"Call the medics," said the first constable. "We don't deal with this kind of shit."

"Or the firefighters," said the second constable. "They can hose him off."

"He should go wash off in The Other Tooth, in their washrooms," said Iqbal.

"No shirt, no trousers, no service," said Bernie, who'd been watching from the sidelines.

"He has a shirt," said Iqbal.

"Hooray. One out of three," said Bernie.

I wondered how much Bernie had paid the beer truck driver to back into Iqbal's trailer.

I turned and walked back to the Herald offices. Klaas would soon be hearing from another set of lawyers.

I smelled the smoke before I rounded the corner. Then I saw it. Thick black smoke from the Herald's windows. Klaas's car was still outside, but he wasn't. The silly mucker must be still in the building.

I put a hurried call through to the fire station then ran in to look for Klaas. I found him on his hands and knees, half passed out from smoke inhalation. Judging by two discarded fire extinguishers near him the old idiot had tried to battle the blaze instead of leaving. And now he was overcome by smoke. I got my hands under his armpits and dragged him towards the exit, his heels dragging on the floor behind us.

He muttered at me all the way, "You total fuck-weasel, you ... sixteen days left... I'd have had it, my life's work ... but you ... you ... had to plug the kettle into the forbidden outlet ... and you let it boil dry ... walked away from it ... let it boil dry... I'll kill you and piss on your grave every day."

I patted him on the arm and said, "Cheer up. You haven't even heard about the lawsuits yet."

Normally I wouldn't have mentioned those, but his ingratitude was getting to me.

He alternated bouts of coughing and swearing at me. "Fucking human wrecking ball. If only Trudie were here. She's the only thing I have to look forward to, now. Thank God she'll be home tomorrow."

Tears were etching snail trails across his soot-blackened cheeks.

Then he passed the maudlin stage and started swearing at me again, he even tried to punch at me as I dragged him to safety.

We emerged—me dragging him out—just as the fire crew, ambulance and Sgt. Panigoniak arrived. They cheered me and clapped me on the shoulders.

"Nicely done," said Panigoniak admiringly. He pointed to the burning building behind me. "Another minute and he'd have been a goner."

Flames were now visible above the building roof. Through the windows I saw sparks as ceiling beams collapsed.

The ambulance men had Klaas on the stretcher. He was making lunging movements at me with his arms and foaming incoherently in Dutch.

When they couldn't calm him, the ambulance crew strapped him to the stretcher. Legs, arms, chest, even his head. He continued shouting, "*Ik ga je vermoorden, moederloze klootzak.*"

They strapped an oxygen mask over his mouth. The shouting became muffled. Hard to understand.

"*Veertig jaar werk en nog maar zestien dagen.*"

Or something like that. Perhaps it was just my imagination. Hard to tell.

One of the ambulance guys turned to me.

"Can you figure out what he's shouting under the mask, Per?"

"Could be 'Happy Birthday' for all I know."

The second ambulance driver was on his radio mike, alerting the hospital, "We've got our load, elderly male, rescued from burning building, smoke inhalation and psychologically disturbed. Resisted rescue. May have set the fire himself. He's singing, 'Happy Birthday.' On our way now."

They left. One wall of the building collapsed.

"Jeez, Per," said Panigoniak. "You went in there to pull him out? Playing hero is going to kill you one of these days."

That was a hard one to answer, in any case I was starting to cough up soot, so I went home to Inge.

"Why are you so grimy, Per?"

"There was a fire at the Naarlen Herald offices."

"Is Klaas OK?"

"He got some smoke inhalation, but otherwise mostly OK."

"Do they know how it started?"

"Bad electrical circuits in an old building, probably."

"Oh, Per, that's so sad. Too bad Trudie's in Lagos. She would have prevented this, or at least been there as a comfort."

"Trudie in Lagos? That's Vietnam, Inge. I thought Trudie was in Africa."

"No, Per. Laos, is Vietnam. Trudie is in Lagos, L-A-G-O-S, Nigeria, Africa."

That stupid, stupid, stupid Klaas. What an absolute moron. Not only had he lived with a ticking time bomb of a shoddy electrical repair for forty years, but, if Inge was right, he'd ruined Trudie's life too. Klaas was such a grade-A fucking disaster area he ruined everybody and everything he touched. Any attempts from me to help him further would be futile. Not that he wanted to speak to me anyway.

"No," I thought to myself, "The best thing you can do, Per, is to wash your hands of Klaas before he ruins your life too. He's the black hole of disasters. Approach too closely and you'll be dragged into his disaster event horizon, never to emerge again. Enough is enough."

That was the end of that, or so I thought. Only, it wasn't. On Saturday, Inge called to me, "Per, one of the Garibaldi hens is loose in our garden."

I grabbed the hen, stuffed her into a box and walked out to the Garibaldi's front door.

Garibaldi Senior answered the door. I held out the hen for him.

He and I have developed a polite formula for this.

"Ah, Per, I'm so sorry she bothered you. I don't know how she gets out."

"Francesco, it's never a bother."

"Let me get you something for your trouble, though."

He disappeared into the recesses of the house. It's always the same, he apologizes and gives me some fresh eggs to take home.

Except, this time it was different.

He came back holding a tiny animal. He held it out to me. I reacted by rote instinct: someone holds out something for you, you hold out your hands in turn. The little animal sat in my palm and stared up at me. It was soft. Its eyes were luminous green. I was scared to drop it. I cupped my hands to my chest to keep it from tumbling off my palms. I could feel the little thing purring. It continued to gaze up at me.

"For you and Inge," said Francesco. "The last of our litter. Eight weeks old today."

I walked home in a trance and sat on the living room sofa with the little thing on my lap. It pressed against me and continued to gaze up at me. I couldn't look away. It held out a paw. I touched the paw with one finger. The little thing purred. We touched paws again. And again. A private game for just the two of us.

Inge shouted to me from the kitchen. When I didn't answer, she sensed something was odd. She came into the living room, froze, rooted like a statue, staring at us. She couldn't take her eyes off the little thing either.

Finally, she held out her arms and said, "Give him to me."

"No."

"WHAT?"

"He's mine."

"No, he isn't, Per. You will give him to me NOW or regret it all your life. I swear it."

“Inge, they are very fragile at this age. They have to be handled calmly, carefully and without emotion, not squeezed, not passed around like a ... like a...”

She took unfair advantage of my search for the mot juste to scoop the kitten off my lap. She headed for the living room exit.

“MINE,” she said. “Not yours.”

In the doorway she hesitated and half turned back to me. “Does he have a name?”

I thought back to the medics putting a neck brace on the groaning engineer; to Edna drumming her handcuffed wrists against the inside of the police car; to the sewage covered figure rising trouserless from the toppled portable toilets; to Councillor Srinivasan shouting that he’d sue The Herald into the ground; to the column of black smoke rising from the collapsing Herald building and to Klaas being driven off in the ambulance.

“Yes,” I said, “his name is Attila.”

“How lovely,” said, Inge. “Attila and I are going to talk. Meanwhile, you will go shopping for his litter box, water bowl, food bowl, cat litter, kitten food, scratching post, leash, cat harness, cat toys, sleeping basket, kitty blanket, brush, comb, an extra carton of full-cream milk, and anything else I may have forgotten. No catnip. He’s too young. After the shopping, you may make lunch for us all. I will let you know at lunch time what your after-lunch duties will be. Until lunch, Attila and I are having private time. We are not to be interrupted.”

There’s no talking to her when she’s in full Queen Boadicea mode. I sighed and went shopping.

*

6. The Mafia Twins

Life in Naarlen is complicated. No surprise; we're seventy-eight degrees north in the Arctic Sea. Months of winter darkness, followed by never-ending day light pivots Naarlanders between suicidal gloom and murderous sleep deficit.

I've said it before, I'll say it again: I'm probably the only sane inhabitant here.

Look at the Coastal Pilot Chartbook for Naarlen. Mariners and navigators use these books to get information about coastlines and anchorages. For Naarlen, the entry says:

> *"Naarlen is one of the few deep-water, sheltered harbours in the surrounding area. It is largely ice-free from June to August. The harbour approach is well marked with buoys, with lights visible from two nautical miles at night. There is a dock with extensive facilities for self-loading vessels up to fifty metres long with drafts up to eight fathoms. Contact the port captain in advance on channel 16 during business hours only. Away from the dock, a rocky bottom at ten fathoms makes anchoring uncertain, but there are ample mooring buoys. Despite the extensive facilities and superior shelter, vessels are advised to avoid Naarlen as the inhabitants are capricious."*

You will not find the word "capricious" used in any other page or volume of the Coastal Pilot series; not for the Arctic, the Med, the Caribbean, the Atlantic, nor even for the Cannibal Islands of Papua New Guinea or Tierra del Fuego. Not once. The Coastal Pilot chooses its words as carefully and concisely as a hanging judge. There must not be the slightest doubt about the sentencing or the outcome. There must be no room for loopholes, quibbles, appeals or differing interpretations. In the case of the Coastal Pilot, mariners' lives depend on the accuracy and clarity of its pronouncements. The difference between rocky bottom at eight fathoms, or sandy bottom at seven fathoms; the difference between sheltered harbour and harbour exposed to north winds, is carefully laid out, page after page, in dry, emotionless tones. Each word is weighed and calibrated. The Coastal Pilot loves precision and measurement. If it adopts a warning tone, the reasons and measurements are always supplied.

> *"Ensure sufficient anchor length. Tidal range may span 14 metres."*
>
> *"Vessels should not attempt to cross the bar at ebb tide. Wave crests as high as seven metres, and troughs with less than one-meter draft may be encountered."*

Even where measurements are elusive, the Coastal Pilot will find them. It is not satisfied with the mere phrase *"Piracy is common along the coast of Bosano."* Instead, it writes, *"Piracy is common for the first one hundred kilometres of coast from Bosanoville northwards.*

In 2020, seventeen incidents were reported, with the furthest from land being one hundred and twenty-five nautical miles offshore."

The phrase *"... inhabitants are capricious..."* without a single explanatory measurement stands alone in the entire series of books and charts, a unique display of emotion that the editors of the series have reserved for only one location in the whole world. Naarlen.

Which leads me to the Mafia twins and Bernie Halloran and the Boreal Penguin.

Francesco is my neighbour. He is a widower bringing up two thirteen-year-old wild boys, known as the Mafia twins.

"Francesco," I said when he knocked on my door one afternoon. "Come in. Come in."

I gave him a cup of coffee. He spoke between sips.

"Per, it's my sister, in Ottawa, she is having a hip operation. I should be there for her. Could you keep an occasional eye on my boys? They're mostly self-sufficient, but if they know they can call on you, and that you will drop by once every couple of days, that would really help. It's also their month for being assistant zookeepers at Christine Nguyen's zoo, so they're quite busy."

I assured him that would be no problem. The boys and I get on well despite their evil reputation.

"Please," said Francesco as he left, "they have annoyed their school principal recently, if you can keep an eye on that too?"

"Sure, Francesco."

The first time I dropped in on the twins, they were doing homework.

"For Principal Lundgren. He's our biology teacher."

"He hates us."

"Dweeb."
"Nerd."
"Dorkus-magnus."
"Fresh-water admiral."
"Tsk, tsk boys."
"Your Norwegian countrymen call him names too."
"Who does, boys?"
"In the 'Dear Maude' column, people wrote that he was a '*drittsekk*.'"
"What does that mean, Mr. Pederson?"
"Is it something bad?"
"Is it mega-rude?"
I ignored their teenage comments. Instead, I asked, "What's your homework for him, boys?"
"We have to pick a biology project. We don't know what to pick." That was from Adriano.
"What do you like to do, boys?"
"Coding on the Internet." That was from Basilio.
"Digital imaging and design." From Adriano.
"Well, boys, if you want Principal Lundgren to hate you less, why not pick something that he's excited about, and do an interesting project with it?"
"Oh."
"Oh."
"So, boys, what does Lundgren like?"
"Nerd stuff."
"Dorkus stuff."
"Dweeb stuff."
"Geriatric dweeb stuff."
"Like what, boys?"
"Birds."
"Bird-watching."
"Sounds like a biology project about birds or bird-watching might be a good idea," I suggested.

I left them to it.

The next time I checked up on the Mafia twins, they weren't home. It was a Saturday afternoon. I remembered what Francesco had told me and found them doing assistant zoo-keeping.

It was face-painting afternoon at the zoo. Adriano and Basilio were painting whiskers and fangs on younger kids using yellow, green, black and white paints. I went over to Christine Nguyen and exchanged hugs with her.

"They're very good with the younger kids," she said, watching the twins happily.

"Are the parents happy to have their young kids painted?"

"It's hypoallergenic paint, Per, and washes off quite easily with soap, hot water and a spoon of persistence."

I went over to the boys.

"Boys, could you paint a realistic moustache and goatee on me?"

"Sure thing, Mr. Pederson."

"You want green and yellow, Mr. Pederson?"

"Thanks, boys. Just black, please."

We chatted while they painted my moustache. The little ones waiting in line were giggling at me.

"How's the project for Lundgren coming along, boys?"

"We took your advice Mr. Pederson. Nerd stuff."

"Geriatric nerdery."

"Something Old Lundgren will like."

As usual they were talking over each other.

"Inge is inviting you over for supper Monday night if you can come, boys. Her calamari specialty."

"Oh, yes, please."

"Yes, please."

"If it's ready we'll show you then, Mr. Pederson."

"See you then boys."

I turned my fur hat inside out, turned my scarf inside out, circled round as though I was just coming through the entrance door, and approached Christine Nguyen again.

"Здравствуй, мое солнышко," I said using one of the few Russian greetings I know. I spread my arms wide to hug her. Something like "Yo, sunshine!"

She stared at my moustache and goatee in puzzlement, then laughed.

"Oh, Per, you got painted! For a moment I couldn't figure out who you were."

She was laughing at my silliness. In reflex reaction to my spread arms, she opened her arms. We hugged, still laughing.

Two hugs from the lovely, lovable Christine for the price of one entrance ticket. I went home with a smile on my face. Don't think for a moment I have Olga-like illusions about Christine and myself. I don't. Apart from the unbridgeable age difference, she dotes on Eberhardt. She's just fun to hug. That's all.

After Inge's dinner on Monday night, the Mafia twins showed me the project they were researching. They opened up a tablet computer they had brought along.

"Look Mr. Pederson, this is the personal web page of Luke Harding."

"You know Luke Harding, Mr. Pederson?"

"No, Adriano."

"He's famous."

"An explorer."

"A naturalist."

"A conservationist."

"An adventurer."

The two boys were again talking over each other in excitement.

"Look at this, Mr. Pederson. Luke sailed a steel-hulled boat through the Northwest Passage last summer."

"He passed the northern end of Naarlen."

"And look what he found."

They showed me a diary entry and a photo from some or other social medium page.

> *"July 20.*
>
> *Wind from the west, variable and light. Open water, very little ice.*
>
> *At 0900 passing Naarlen, I caught a glimpse of a bird most ornithologists believe has been extinct since the 1800s. The Boreal Penguin. Pygoscelis borealis. The only penguin to have existed in the Northern Hemisphere. All other penguins are Southern Hemisphere creatures.*
>
> *I can't be sure, the rocks around Naarlen prevent me sailing closer and my photo is grainy. However, the yellow underbill, and green stripe under the wings match the few early descriptions of the species.*
>
> *How I wish I could come back another year to scout Naarlen more closely for another view of this creature."*

"Fascinating," I said to the boys. "If that doesn't grab Mr. Lundgren's attention, I don't know what will. When do you hand in your project?"

"Friday," said Adriano.

"End of term," said Basiliano.

"Start of holidays."

"Good luck with the project, boys," I said. "It looks like a winner."

The next Saturday, I went back to the zoo. It doesn't open until late afternoon on Saturdays. That gives the zoo keepers time in the morning to get things thoroughly cleaned out.

I found Adriano alone at the zoo polishing the brass signs saying, "Alpaca (The Andes, Chile)" and "Cape Penguin (The South Atlantic, South Africa)."

I didn't see either animal, but maybe they move them when they're hosing down the enclosures.

"Where's Basilio?" I asked. It was the first time I'd seen one Mafia Twin without the other.

Adriano looked uncomfortable at this. Maybe they're not used to being apart.

"He'll be here later, Mr. Pederson."

"Oh. And what did Lundgren think of your project?"

"He looked at the Luke Harding photo of the bird, and got very excited by it. He thinks it's the real thing, a rediscovered boreal penguin. He said he'd go up to the north end of the island himself this morning. He hopes to see one. He says that would make him the second person this century to see the bird. He's very, very excited."

"Oh. He didn't offer to take you boys with, him? After all you did to make him aware of this."

"No, Mr. Pederson."

Well, that's Lundgren for you. No decency, not with birds and not with his poker debts.

I nodded to Adriano, and left him to his sign polishing.

Things snowballed rapidly from there.

Lundgren came back from his Saturday morning survey of the northern end of Naarlen with another grainy picture of what might have been a penguin with a yellow underbill and green stripes under the wings. Again, the photo was from a great distance, but that did nothing to diminish Lundgren's excitement.

Within days he'd shared Luke Harding's material, and his own photo of the strange bird with his cousin, Professor Lundgren, at the Uppsala Royal Institute for Swedish Ornithology.

Enormous excitement followed. The Uppsala Institute organized a field trip of four professors to fly out to Naarlen. Lundgren—that is our Lundgren—was sworn to silence because no academic wants to share the glory of rediscovering a species with a crowd of other academics. Publish first, or perish first.

None the less the story, and the excitement soon made the rounds in Naarlen, because our Lundgren can't keep a secret.

Bernie Halloran cornered me at The Other Tooth.

"A coffee in private with you, please Per."

He took me to the back room.

"I hear you're keeping an eye on the Mafia boys, while Francesco is out of town?"

"That's right, Bernie."

"Do they get on with Principal Lundgren?"

"Not well, at least until this week."

"Bit of animosity was there, Per? I mean from the boys for Lundgren."

"Ja, ja. They don't like Lundgren."

"This Luke Harding, the yachtsman, you know much about him or his followers?"

"No. I don't do social media."

"It's funny. His following is growing rapidly, as though he's only recently become well known. I asked Naarlen Telecom to tell me about the IP addresses of Luke and his followers. A lot of Naarlen IP addresses, Per."

"I don't speak Internet, Bernie. Means nothing to me."

"The photo, Per, the Luke Harding photo of the bird is interesting too. I spent a while looking at it under a magnifying glass. Interesting. Have you looked at it?"

"Not much to see, Bernie. Luke does admit he was too far away for good identification. Would have been better if he could have sailed closer."

Bernie nodded. Then he changed direction.

"It's a big thing these professors coming to Naarlen, Per. I want to make sure their trip is successful. Be good for the town, good for the tourist industry on Naarlen. I might even add some hotel rooms next to the pub if this bird thing takes off."

"Hard to guarantee anyone a successful trip, isn't it, Bernie? I mean, it's up to the birds if they show themselves. The north end is rugged coastline, the bay, the rocks, the ice floes. Not easy going, and you can't get close by sea. Easy to overlook a bird here or there, unless they're present in big numbers."

He gave me one of those long looks that he specializes in. I never understand them.

Then he nodded. "That's so, Per. Have to do our best to make sure the bird shows itself. Do you mind if I drop in on the boys a bit while Francesco's away? Take some of the load off you?"

"Sure, Bernie. No problem."

The professors arrived on a Friday. On Saturday morning they visited the area where our Lundgren had spotted the possible boreal penguin. At the same time as they were bird hunting, I dropped into the zoo to check on the Mafia twins.

I found Basilio alone hosing down the Alpaca pen.

"Where's Adriano, I'm not used to seeing either one of you without the other?"

Again, the single twin looked uneasy.

"He'll be back later, Mr. Pederson. Bernie Halloran took Adriano bird-watching. But one of us has to stay to clean the zoo before opening time. We couldn't both go."

I nodded. "Call me if you boys need anything."

Within an hour or two, the town was abuzz. News was that the professors had several glimpses of a single boreal penguin, but only from afar. Whenever they got close to where the bird had last been sighted, it disappeared and popped up even further away, half obscured by a rock outcrop or hills.

Bernie dropped in on me later in the same day.

"Just letting you know, I borrowed Adriano this morning, but have dropped him off next door. He's back home now."

"Thanks, Bernie. I hear you and Adriano were searching for boreal penguins too this morning. Same time as the professors. Bit of competition between you and the professors? Did you see anything?"

"Didn't see a thing, Per. Not even a feather. Didn't see the professors either, though we must have been in the same area."

"Bit of a wasted trip, then Bernie?"

"Yer."

"What now, Bernie?"

"Got to drop by the professors and ensure they understand that Naarlen is a dangerous environment for newcomers. Polar bear season. And the ice is thin in places. Got to make 'em understand not to go out without letting the town know ahead of time. Got to tell 'em to take a guide that's armed for bear."

In spite of Bernie's warning, there was an upset on the Monday morning. I heard about it afterwards from Bernie, in the Other Tooth. He used one of those English idioms that give me so much trouble.

"You can take a Norse to the water, but you can't make 'im think."

I tried it slowly to see if it would make more sense.

"You can take a Norse to water..."

It didn't make sense. "What does it mean, Bernie?"

"Means that one of the profs, Lundgren's cousin—no surprise there—decided to ignore my advice. Went out by himself to North Bay. Tried to get the jump on his colleagues."

"Oh."

"You know how difficult the beach walk is with the cliffs and all. He went out on the sea ice to get around the cliffs. The chunk of ice he was on broke free and there he was floating in the bay with nothing more than a camera, cell phone and binoculars."

"Did he know how Naarlen Telecom works?"

"Wowza, Per, does anyone?"

In the rest of Canada, if you have an emergency you dial 911. A dispatcher answers the phone and asks what your emergency is and whether you need police, fire or ambulance. That may work in towns down south, but it fails miserably in Naarlen.

In Naarlen, almost everyone knows almost everyone. As a result, a 911 call in Naarlen used to go like this.

"This is 911, please state your emergency."

"Oh, this is Betty, I thought Alvin was on duty today?"

"Oh, hi Betty, it's Jolene."

"Hi, Jolene. So, where's Alvin?"

"We swapped shifts."

"Just as well I caught you Jolene; while I've got you, can I ask about your plum tart recipe."

"Did you try it?"

"It was delicious, but it sagged in the middle."

"How long did you let it rise before putting it into the oven."

"About forty-five minutes."

"Hmm. Is your kitchen warm."

"Oh, yes, since Barry reinsulated."

"I should get Jon to do that for us. Anyway, forty-five minutes is too long. Try thirty minutes next time. And how is Barry?"

"Hang on, let me check ... ah... I see him ... not so good, Jolene. He's still on lying face down, coughing. It's kind of why I called 911."

"Oh, do you want an ambulance then, Betty?"

"Actually, I wanted the firefighters, but let me take another gander ... no ... no point in the firefighters anymore. The workshop has just about burnt to the ground now. Not much left to save by the time they get here."

"Oh. Too bad. Maybe an ambulance then? For Barry coughing?"

"No, thanks Jolene, it's just the smoke. He's used to that. Still a pack-a-day man, you know."

"I thought he was going to quit?"

"Didn't happen. Anyway, I'll try the thirty-minute rise for the plum tart and let you know. Nice chatting, Jolene, I should probably let you get back to your other calls."

"True, I've got another two on hold, Betty."

"Well, you keep well, Jolene."

"You too, Betty, be sure to let me know about the plum tart."

After too many of these emergency calls gone wrong, the Naarlen city council instituted a new emergency phone system. In Naarlen now, you do NOT dial 911 for an emergency. You dial straight through to whichever emergency service you need, cutting out the middleman or middle-woman. There's no more chitchat with a dispatcher asking you which emergency service you need. The numbers to dial are easy to remember:

- Dialling 666 for an ambulance sounds like sick, sick, sick.
- Dialling 555 for fire sounds like fire, fire, fire.
- Dialling 888 for poison-control sounds like ate, ate, ate.
- Dialling 999 for police sounds like nein, nein, nein.

Unfortunately, the French-speaking contingent on Naarlen still dial 555 for boating emergencies—cinq, cinq, cinq—which makes no sense, but that's Anglo-French language politics for you.

911 is no longer an emergency number. It's the top-ten hits of the week music sponsored by ads from a luxury sports car company. It's a popular phone number with teenagers.

Naarlen council, selected for their plodding, linear thought processes by Bernie, wanted to reserve 333 for tree's falling on roads and houses, and 222 for train derailments. Bernie reminded them Naarlen has neither trees nor trains.

"So, Bernie," I said. "To continue. Here's the professor, cousin to our own Lundgren, floating on the bay and no clue how to call emergency services. What happened?"

"He listened to top-ten hits. At first, he thought he was getting music while on hold for a 911 dispatcher."

"Must have gotten a mighty cold bum, Bernie."

"Yer. He says he's not a pop music fan anyway, except Abba. Anyway, then the car advertisements came on. He drives a Volvo back home and thinks Porsche is German nonsense. So, he gave up on 911 and called his cousin—our Lundgren."

I'd already heard that part from our Lundgren's school secretary, the delightful Jane Hennerman. She dislikes our Lundgren, the school principal, almost as much as I do.

She wasn't aware that one of the visiting professors was also a Lundgren. She was understandably confused when she answered the school phone and a voice said, "Ja. This is Lundgren. I need help."

"Yes, Mr. Lundgren. What is it?"

"I'm floating on ice."

"In your office? Floating? On nice what?"

"What office?"

"Your office, Mr. Lundgren."

"Is Lundgren there?"

"Did you take your medication this morning, Mr. Lundgren?"

"What medication? This is Lundgren. Is Lundgren there. I need help."

"Is that Mr. Lundgren calling?"

"Ja, ja. Please put me through to Lundgren."

"Please, hold."

She put down the receiver and walked across to our Lundgren's office.

"Did you just call me, Mr. Lundgren?"

"No. Why?"

"There's a lunatic on the phone that wants to speak to you."

"A lunatic?"

"Yes."

Jane told me Lundgren looked anxious. After all, he's a school principal. He sees himself as an important man, a leader of tomorrow's youth, he shouldn't have to deal with the unexpected, his life should be routine clockwork. In his view, anyway.

"Get rid of him, Jane. I don't want to speak to lunatics."

"Of course, Mr. Lundgren."

Jane went back to the phone and said to the other Lundgren, "Sorry to keep you waiting, I'm putting you through to Mr. Lundgren now."

Now I wanted to hear the rest from Bernie.

He continued:

"Lundgren—our Lundgren—called me. I went out with the Harbour Police on their Zodiac-cum-ice-sled. We pulled the professor off the ice and boated him back all the way around the island to Naarlen Harbour."

"Jeez, Bernie, the long way round. Why? You could have waded out from North Bay shore and walked him back. North Bay's barely calf deep, unless he'd floated beyond the sand bar."

"Tourism," Bernie said to me and winked. "If we had waded him back to shore, he would have been embarrassed, and hated us. This way, with the long boat trip, he has a story to tell. This way, he's a brave arctic explorer, the envy of his colleagues, a story that he can embellish for years. He'll throw in storms, fog, giant waves and polar bears. Plus, it underlines for him and his colleagues the importance of using paid guides. We can now upsell what used to be a walk on the beach into dangerous guided expeditions."

"Seriously?"

"Seriously, is right, Per. To underline the seriousness of Professor Lundgren's foolhardiness and near-death experience, I've banned the four professors from the island for the rest of the season. They have to pay the cost of Professor Lundgren's very expensive rescue and I've put them on a plane for Iqaluit, leaving tonight. Banned for the season."

"For heaven's sake, Bernie. Why?"

"I'm turning Naarlen into Mount Everest, Bernie. If any idiot can stroll on a beach by himself and look for a bird, they'll send one miserable postgrad student next year. The postgrad will live on the beach in a tent and eat nothing but cheap granola and canned ravioli. No contribution to our tourism economy. Nobody else will come. You can stroll on beaches anywhere in the world.

But, if I make the professors apply for an expedition permit, like Mount Everest, they'll send a fully equipped team of twenty and hire our guides, buy our freeze-dried food, rent our Zodiac boats, tents, stoves, rescue gear, armed guards, Inuit interpreters, polar-bear-sniffing dogs, trail cameras, infrared cameras, ornithology hides, lagoon waders, chefs, and arctic-all-weather drone cameras. And the other universities will do the same. Everest tourism, Bernie, that's what I'm doing. They're leaving on the plane tonight, but they'll be drooling to come back next season. They've had a glimpse of what might be an extinct bird, and they can't wait to confirm it. Even if the expedition permits are expensive. And they will be."

"Will be what, Bernie?"

"Expensive. The permits will be expensive to target the high-end market and limit the numbers."

"What?"

"It's like watches, Bernie. You can buy an accurate watch for fifteen dollars. But if you want to target the wealthy, you have to charge two thousand dollars, even though the watch won't be as accurate as the fifteen-dollar model. Snob appeal. Our North Bay expedition permits will have snob appeal for universities. Who else can boast of a beach holiday with a $7,000 expedition permit and armed guide?"

"Without sun, sand, warm water or bikinis."

"Doesn't matter to academics," said Bernie.

He unfolded a sheet of architectural plans for a hotel he wanted to build.

"Look at my plans, Per."

Alarms were going off in my head.

"Not now, Bernie." I held up a hand.

He paused. "What?"

"Det er ugler i mosen, Bernie."

"Is that Norwegian, Per?"

"Yes. You English have idioms. Like taking a Norse to water. We Norwegians have 'Det er ugler i mosen.'"

"I'm Australian Per, not English. Anyway, what's that supposed to mean?"

"Translated into English, Bernie, it means there are owls in the moss."

"Really? Does that happen often in Norway? Owls in the moss?"

"It's an expression that means something is wrong."

"Oh. In English we say something is rotten in Denmark, Per."

"Nei, nei, that is not an idiom, Bernie. That is just the boring truth about Denmark. Ask any Norwegian child. Or even a Swedish child. The only child who doesn't know is a Danish child. Now I go to find the owls in the moss."

It was time to check on the Mafia twins. School holidays. They were both at the zoo again. I found them. And I found something else. It wasn't pretty. It confirmed my worst suspicions. Owls in the moss. I went back to see Bernie.

"Bernie, another word privately please?"

We went into his back room.

"What, Per? Did you find your owls?"

"Yes. You need to put all your Everest tourism plans on hold. And the construction of your luxury hotel."

"Yer?"

"I was down at Christine Nguyen's zoo."

"Oh, yer, not much of a zoo for a man in the luxury tourism business, right? Just one alpaca and a Cape penguin."

"The Mafia twins are assistant zoo keepers this month. You knew, of course."

Bernie looked uneasy. He waggled one hand like a shark fin with Parkinsons.

"I think you can guess what I found, Bernie."

Bernie made sure that the door behind us was firmly closed. He lowered his voice.

"I'm guessing you'll tell me what you found, Per."

"The Mafia twins. They were washing yellow paint off the Cape penguin's underbill, and cleaning green paint stripes off its wings."

"Were they? That's odd, Per."

"Not really, Bernie. I reckon they manufactured the Luke Harding, sailor and adventurer, website out of thin air, and took grainy photos of the zoo penguin with paint on. Just to get at Principal Lundgren. And then Basilio let Principal Lundgren get a distant glimpse and photo of the same creature when Lundgren scouted North Bay."

"Interesting theory, Per, but the four professors also saw Boreal penguins out near North Bay..."

"Nei, nei. They didn't see penguins, plural. They saw one penguin, over and over, from a distance. The same morning you took Adriano out there. I'm guessing with the painted Cape penguin, yet again. One that you lifted briefly above a rock here and there, just long enough for the professors to get a glimpse. While keeping yourself and Adriano hidden."

Bernie looked pained

"Now, Per, how can you believe ...?"

"Bernie, show me your hands please."

"What?"

"Show me your hands, please, Bernie."

He lifted his hands. We both stared at the green and yellow paint marks on his hands.

He lifted his shoulders.

"Per, I need you to keep this quiet..."

"Bernie, it's deceit."

"Nah, Per. It's just a bit of fun with the Mafia twins. Building on their original prank against Principal Lundgren. They're enterprising kids. It will be good for the town's economy. They're my junior partners in the hotel."

"It's deceit, crookery, turning the boys into fraudsters and villains. And it will also look bad for Christine Nguyen and her zoo project. Deceit."

"Nah, Per, no more deceit than you pretending to be Aunt Maude."

That stopped me.

"You know about that?"

"'Course, Per. You can rely on my silence, though. Just like I hope I can rely on yours."

I hesitated. He continued.

"Look Per, Old Man Garibaldi has left you in charge of the boys. When he comes back, you can either tell him everything's fine, they did a great biology project, Principal Lundgren loves them, they were good zoo assistants, they're helping me with a hotel project, they may have helped with a historic rediscovery, or..."

"Or?"

"Or you can tell their father that they fabricated their biology homework, that they've been expelled from school, that the four professors are suing them for fraud, and that they're banned as zoo assistants. And it all happened while you were in charge. Also, they may face time in a juvenile corrections centre down south for the fraud charges."

I hesitated again. Then Bernie threw in a clincher.

"I could put in a good word for you with Olga, Per."

"How's this going to work, Bernie? I mean once the professors get a clear photo to convince them the bird exists, or to convince them the bird is a fake, either way the tourism flood is over, right?"

Bernie waggled his head.

"Do you know how lotteries work, Bernie?"

"Some lucky person buys a winning ticket and hits the jackpot."

"You're looking at it the wrong way, Per. Lotteries don't make money by selling winning tickets. They make money by selling thousands and thousands of losing tickets. They give away just enough money to keep the losers coming back for more."

"And?"

"And I'll do that with the penguin. The universities will NOT get a conclusive photo of the penguin. They'll glimpse just enough far-off penguins to keep them coming back for more. Year after year. When one university gives up, another will take over."

"I see."

I considered. Bernie can be a bastard. But my duty was not to myself or even bettering relations with Olga, although civic duty dictated I should try for better relations there too. Nei, nei. That was not the priority. My duty was to the boys. In loco parentis as the lawyers say.

"Here's my counteroffer then, Bernie. I'll keep quiet one condition."

"Yer?"

"The Mafia twins and Christine. I don't want them involved further in anything that could get them or the zoo into trouble. I'm fine with the twins being junior partners in any honest hotel scheme, but not in painting penguins for you. That's my condition."

He thought. Then held out a hand. Reluctantly.

"Fine Per, I'll find someone else to work with. An adult. And it won't involve Christine and her zoo or her animals either. That suit you?"

We shook on the deal.

"And," I added, "I'm not doing this for Olga."

"Right, Per," he said. "So, I shouldn't say anything to her?"

"I didn't say that, Bernie. In a small community like ours, it is always best to mend fences."

He winked in an offensive manner.

I have dignity; whatever Bernie was implying with the wink, I ignored. I walked to the zoo. I had a long conversation with Adriano and Basilio.

It didn't go well initially.

"It's your fault, Mr. Pederson."

"You're the one who said we had to do a project on birds."

"We have almost no birds in the Arctic."

"None that are interesting."

"So we HAD to invent something."

"Only because you made us do it."

"You didn't say we couldn't invent."

"When we do essays for Mr. Kritzinger in English class, he likes us to invent."

"He says imagination is a gift."

"Not a crime."

"It's not our fault."

I wagged my finger at them, swore them to silence and better behaviour. I confiscated the yellow and green paints and threw those into a dumpster on my way home to Inge.

Francesco was in our living room, having tea and cake with Inge. He rose to greet me.

"Per, I'm back. How are you, I hope the boys were no trouble?"

"None, Francesco. They did a great biology project for Lundgren. He loves them. They're down at the zoo right now tending to the animals. Should be home soon. Everything is fine. I hope your sister is good too."

He smiled. "She is. But I'm so relieved about the boys, Per. I know they can be a bit wild, but they're good boys at heart. I knew if anyone in this town could keep them in line while I was gone it was you. *Mille, mille grazie*. I'm so relieved. I don't think anyone else could have done it. I'm lucky to have you as a neighbour, Per. I don't care what the rest of the town says about you, Per, Naarlen is lucky to have you."

He had tears in his eyes. I mumbled something in embarrassment and looked down to give him time to wipe his eyes. Which gave me time consider.

Life is odd, no? Sometimes I do heroic things, like attempting to rescue Olga or Klaas, at great risk to myself, and they swear at me. Refuse to speak to me, even. Thankless shits, both of them. Today, though, I'd done something that felt dishonest, yet Francesco was thanking me. For lying to him. For covering up. Worse, it was me who'd suggested the disastrous biology project to the boys.

I paused to consider further.

Certainly, the project had won their principal's approval. Point in my favour. True, the boys had veered from the straight and narrow, but that was because of Bernie Halloran. Another point in my favour. And I was the one who'd nipped Bernie's fraud in the bud, and set the boys back on the right path. Not an easy task, and few others in Naarlen could have done it as well.

A longer pause. Why was I saying, "Few others in Naarlen could have done it?"

Nei, nei. No one else in Naarlen could have done it. Big point in my favour. And I had saved the lovely Christine and her zoo from a large embarrassment. Huge point in my favour. She would never know what I'd done for her, but I deserved another dozen hugs from her. I began to feel better.

Francesco *was* correct: I'd been just as much a hero as the other times. Naarlen *was* lucky to have me.

I looked up and smiled. Inge was standing next to me proudly. Her arm was around my waist. Inge knows. Inge appreciates what I do for others. I love Inge. She is the smartest woman I know. I would have liked to ask Inge about whether and how I should collect a dozen hugs from Christine. Inge understands women, but explaining it all to Inge might be complicated. She's a birdwatcher. If I told her about owls in the moss, she'd get sidetracked. She'd ask what kind of owls, what kind of moss, and was it in breeding season. I'd have to forgo her advice this time.

"You're welcome, Francesco," I said humbly, and escorted him to the door.

*

7. The Goose With a Pearl Earring

Naarlen was a German Arctic colonial territory until the end of WWI. This surprises people. I remind them that Alaska was once a Russian colony, sold to the USA in 1867.

Naarlen's natural history is as odd as its political history. The world's only Northern Hemisphere penguin, the Boreal penguin, was thought to have been hunted into extinction for its beautiful green wing feathers. It was last seen in the 1800s. Recent photographs, though inconclusive, have fuelled hope it may still be alive and breeding on the northern tip of Naarlen.

Arts and culture, unfortunately, are a blank page for Naarlen. There is no record of any Inuit settlement on Naarlen before German colonization. The German colonists produced only the "Flaschenberg," the mountain of accumulated empty beer bottles to the west of Naarlen Township. Beer was shipped to Naarlen from Germany, but cost prevented the empties being shipped back. The empties accumulated in the Flaschenberg—the "Bottle Mountain." Canadian rule post WWI built up the Flaschenberg further, but did not add culture. Naarlen is not known for Inuit whalebone carving, nor for any homegrown Rembrandt's, Picassos, Rodins, Bachs, Beethovens, Oliviers, Lorcas, Nureyevs or Pavlovas.

Which was why I was surprised to see Bernie Halloran studying a book of Johannes Vermeer paintings in The Other Tooth. The Other Tooth serves up cold beer, stale peanuts, reasonably hot chips, lukewarm drunks and fresh puke. It's not a natural environment for old Dutch masters.

Bernie, our mayor and consummate politician, is full of surprises, though.

"What Naarlen needs, Per, is a culture festival."

"A what?"

"Maybe on Canada Day, July first."

"And Vermeer? How does he fit into this, Bernie?"

"Of all the grandmasters, he's my favourite, my inspiration for this. Just look at this, Per."

He opened his book to a full-page image of Vermeer's "Girl with a Pearl Earring."

"1665, Per, and you'll never see a portrait done better, not on canvas, not in camera, not in cinema. Look at the contrasts between bright and dark. Look at how he uses the highlights and shadows for dramatic effect. Look at how many shades of blue he captures in her headdress. You can *feel* the texture of the cloth. He's fabulous."

"Bernie, there's a problem. For your culture festival ..."

"What's that, mate?'

"Vermeer won't come to the festival. He's dead. You know that, right?"

Bernie slapped me on the back. "He's just the inspiration, you drongo, you. Naarlen has plenty of aspiring artists that deserve recognition."

"Who, Bernie?"

"We have a very strong group of kayak builders, including your friend Panigoniak. Their boats are works of art. Whalebone, sea lion skins, and caribou antler. Who else: we have Grandma Mac at the Naarlen and General Savings Co-Op and..."

"Grandma Mac? What has she ever done Bernie, except nearly getting me killed?"

"Grandma Mac reads and tells stories to the children at the library every Friday. Didn't you know, Per? Marvellous recitations and stories. Then, we have the women's group that spin alpaca wool and knit the most wonderful sweaters. If the Shetlands has its distinctive sweater pattern, why not a world-famous Naarlen sweater pattern? Also, there's Olga."

"Olga? Ungrateful turd. I saved her life and she won't talk to me."

"I know, Per. I'm still working on that. Just be patient."

"And what's she done artistically?"

"She runs a small studio producing the most fabulous fashion designs in silk and sealskin. She gets orders from across the globe. Very exclusive work. For millionaires only. A set of her gloves will cost you six months' salary. And her caribou and sealskin jackets are the envy of the world. You couldn't afford them. They sell out every season."

"Huh."

"And we have a sprinkling of musicians and painters too."

"Like who, Bernie?"

"Like the miners' choir up at Naarlen Coal. Gives you goosebumps to listen to them. Have you heard them sing in the colliery main shaft? The acoustics are better than any concert hall. And how about Kristoff and Anna Huygens who have the shack overlooking the seal meat cannery? He paints oils. She does ceramic sculpture."

"Come on, Bernie. Kristoff's been working on his vision for twenty years. And Anna on hers. Neither has ever sold a piece. They keep destroying their work and starting over every two or three years for as long as anyone can remember."

"Confidentially, Per, they're both close to finishing this time around. I've seen their current work and it's fabulous. Either one on their own could steal the show. Their work is simply outstanding. World class. You should take a look. My point is the list of Naarlen arts and culture people is long. I could go on and on."

"You're going to put it to city council, Bernie? The idea of a culture festival?"

"It's on the agenda for Monday evening's meeting. Come along and listen. We welcome citizen comments."

On Monday evening, Councillor Iqbal Srinivasin was the only one to oppose the idea of a Canada Day culture festival.

"Madam Chair," he said in council, "this is another one of Mayor Halloran's fiscal follies. I challenge the Mayor to present a well-thought-out budget for his proposal, rather than some half-baked notion."

Bernie rose.

"Madam Chair, Councillor Srinivasin may not have any patriotic feelings for Canada Day, the day that marks our nation's confederation. But he is the exception. Fellow councillors, we shouldn't, nay, we cannot let the day go unmarked. How do we explain that the rest of our country has celebrations, fireworks, art displays, sporting tournaments, yet we Naarlenders let the day go unmarked because one lone, unpatriotic holdout of a councillor is concerned with his bookkeeping?"

Bernie sat. Srinivasin rose. He was visibly annoyed.

"I am a fourth-generation Canadian. My forefathers fought in the Canadian armed forces..."

Here was another English idiom to puzzle me.

"Four fathers?" I said out loud. "Nei, nei, how is that possible?"

I hadn't meant to say it aloud. Iqbal heard me. He gave me an evil look. For a moment he lost the thread of his discourse. Then, with visible effort, he took his eyes off me and restarted.

"... I am a fourth-generation Canadian. My forefathers fought in the Canadian armed forces in both world wars and then in Korea. Now, now, this Australian fugitive, Halloran, and this escapee from Norway, want to lecture me on Canadian patriotism. How is this possible?"

Bernie rose. Bernie too had heard my comment. He made the most of it, but then, Bernie would. He'd give even Loki a run for his money.

"Madam Chair. My heart goes out to Councillor Srinivasin. I can only imagine the difficult childhood he had, not being able to narrow down his paternity beyond four potential fathers. And one can only imagine the embarrassment he felt for his mother. It makes me truly appreciate the stability of my own parental home and my parent's fidelity to each other. In support of Councillor Srinivasin's difficult situation, I note that the stigma of not knowing who one's real father is, is thankfully no longer as ugly as it once was."

Council discussions became heated about then. The angry looks that Srinivasin directed at me became so intense that I left. The outcome of the council debate was never in doubt anyway. Bernie would organize a culture festival for Naarlen on July first. He has a handpicked, compliant council.

Later that week, I dropped in on Kristoff and Anna Huygens for a cup of coffee and to view the state of their work. Anna's ceramic sculpture was of a snow goose in flight. I was polite about it, but in truth I couldn't see the attraction. It must be difficult to represent something as airborne and graceful as a snow goose in flight with lumpish, dense clay hacked and gouged from heavy, earthbound soil. Anna had managed to make it look less like a goose and more like a cross between a pregnant hippopotamus and a constipated vulture. Of course, we Norwegians are polite; I kept that thought to myself.

It was harder to be polite about Kristoff's work. I liked it even less than Anna's hippo-vulture.

"I call it 'Tranquility 46', Per."

"Ja, ja. Tranquility. Obviously," I lied. "But why 46?"

"It's my forty-sixth attempt at capturing the spirit of the land. And this time I've done it. Each time I've tried a different technique—everything from Zen meditation to Psilocybe mushroom tea—to break past my self-imposed creative barriers. And now, my forty-sixth attempt, I'm finally in touch with my true inner voice. I've finally been able to liberate my inner vision of this land in the way I've always dreamed."

"This tea, Kristoff, this is not ...?"

"No, no. Rest easy, Per. That was a failure. Way back at 'Tranquility 23.' You're drinking normal Ceylon tea."

"Oh, good. So, what method did you use to unlock vision number 46?"

"It took so much out of me, Per. I couldn't do it again."

"O, o, I would not allow it again," said Anna, fondly. "It almost killed him. O, o, I was so concerned."

"What was it, Kristoff?"

"An old first-nation method, Per. I starved myself for two weeks."

"O, o," said Anna. "I was dead against it. A miracle he survived."

"For two weeks Per, only hot water. No other food or drink. And I wandered the shores of Naarlen, day and night with a sketch book, waiting for inspiration."

"Do you remember how weak I became, Anna?"

"O, o, I was scared for you, Kristoff. You could barely walk. You staggered."

"Anna's right, Per. I fell into a trance state. A dream world. When the inspiration finally came, I was so weak I could barely hold a pencil to my sketch book, yet the results were worth it. A once-in-a-lifetime gift. I can never repeat the ordeal, it would kill me, but it was worth it. What do you think?"

"I'm stunned," I said, which was true. How can a man make forty-six attempts at something, starve himself in the cause, and still come up with something so mediocre?

Anna and Kristoff nodded.

"I knew you'd appreciate it. When Anna told me you were dropping by, I said you'd appreciate it. Didn't I, Sweets?"

"O, yes," said Anna. "O, yes. That's exactly what Kristoff said to me. O, exactly that."

Inge has some women's magazines at home. I looked at one once. It discussed how difficult it is for some women to achieve an "O." Anna seemed to have perfected it. It's not difficult for Norwegian speakers, but then again some of my countrymen have trouble with the English "th" sound. Would an "O" be more difficult for Dutch speakers? Does the "O" sound even get used in Dutch? The only other Dutch speaker I know is Klaas van Vuuren. He'd once shouted at me, "Ik ga je vermoorden, moederloze klootzak."

There were no "O" sounds in there, so perhaps it is challenging for Dutch women—and maybe men too—to achieve the sound, just like Inge's magazine said. Then again, Klaas was speaking through an oxygen mask, which muffled his speech.

"So, you like it then?" said Kristoff, interrupting my language analysis.

"It's unbelievable," I said, hoping Kristoff would read more into that than I meant.

They both smiled happily.

"Tell me, Kristoff, your technique, I've never seen an artist use such large paint pots, instead of artists' tubes of paint. It's the same size paint pots I use for painting walls."

"You're correct Per. I have developed my own techniques to match the size of my canvas."

I gazed at the vast canvas. It was at least six metres wide and 2 metres high—about 18 feet wide and six feet high. It was painted mostly in shades of gray with only minute touches of colour showing through the gray here and there.

Kristoff hastened to educate me.

"I use the bright colours as underlay, then paint over them in gray. Then I repeat. Colour and again gray. It gives a very subtle effect. Big brushes, big paint pots, sometimes a paint roller, no fiddling with small tubes of paint. My vision is too large."

"Ah," I said, then changed it to "Oh," and smiled supportively at Anna.

"Unique. Unique, Kristoff. I've never seen the like."

Anna interjected. "O Per, did you know my goose is iterative also? I build up one layer of goose, bake the ceramic, then add another layer of clay around that core, bake it again, and so on. Layer after layer, shell after shell, like a Russian egg. Kristoff and I, we both have the same approach. O Per, isn't that wonderful?"

I nodded in a way that I hoped would indicate my appreciation for their genius, and Anna's language abilities. I thanked them for the tea and left.

I dropped in on Bernie at The Other Tooth. I was going to tell him how god-awful the Huygen's art was, but he spoke first. After that, I didn't have the heart.

"Guess what, Per?"

"What, Bernie?"

"You know I have contacts all over the world, at all levels?"

It was true. Bernie's friend, the German State Secretary for Foreign Affairs, had visited Naarlen and got the German Government to pay for our new harbour bridge.

"Ja, ja, contacts."

"Well, Per, I have invited the curators from Italy's Uffizi gallery, from Britain's Tate gallery, and my old friend Mr. Takahashi from the Towada gallery in Japan to come to our Naarlen Culture Day. And they've all accepted. I'm over the moon. I can't wait for them to see the Huygens's art. And of course, our other events."

"Oy, Bernie."

I had a deep sense of foreboding about July first in Naarlen.

"Listen, Per, I want our VIP guests to be well looked after while they're here. Will you escort Mr. Takahashi during our culture day? Tag along with him, answer any questions he has, keep him happy, make sure he has a good time and such?"

"Ja, ja. Well, sure. I will keep him happy."

July first came and things went with surprising rapidity from merely uncomfortable to full-on survival mode.

Mr. Takahashi somehow slipped away from me to listen to Grandma Mac reading children's stories. Then he found me again and was full of questions.

"Mr. Pederson, why do you call her Grandma? She is young."

He held out his smartphone and showed me the video he'd filmed of the library session. I peered at the video. Councillor Iqbal was introducing the reader.

"I regret to say, Grandma Mac has taken ill. I have found a great replacement, Naarlen's own veterinary, Konnie."

I groaned. Konnie is known in Naarlen as "Foulmouth Konnie." Only a klutz of the first water, only Iqbal, would have chosen her to read children's stories. Unless he was deliberately sabotaging Bernie's event.

"Ja, ja, Mr. Takahashi, I see..."

"Please Mr. Pederson, you must call me Akito. Please."

He bowed.

I bowed. "Thank you, you must call me Per."

We shook hands and bowed one more time.

"Akito, ..."

He bowed again. "Yes. Now we are friends, Per. You used my name. I used yours. In Japan this would be a big moment. We would toast each other with hot saki."

I bowed too and said, "We will have a coffee together then, Akito. Soon."

Then I restarted the answer to his original question.

"Akito, I see from your video that Grandma McKenzie was sick."

"Ah."

"She was replaced by a younger woman called Konnie."

"Ah. And this younger woman, Konnie, she read a poem about three little kittens."

"Ja, ja, Akito. In English, it is a well-known story:

"Three little kittens have lost their mittens and they began to cry, oh Mother dear we greatly fear our mittens we have lost."

"Yes, that was the one Per. What are mittens and why do kittens have them?"

"Akito, mittens are like gloves."

"Yes?"

"And when a cat, or a kitten, has different colour fur on its feet, say a black cat with white paws, that looks like the cat is wearing gloves or mittens."

"Ah. I see. And why did the kittens lose their mittens?"

"Akito, sometimes cats, or kittens, sit with their front legs tucked under their chest. When they sit like that, then you cannot see their paws, their mittens. You might say they've lost their mittens."

"Ah. Per, you are a good explainer. Western culture is not easy for Japanese. Now, explain please, why does the mother cat get angry."

"Does she, Akito?"

"Oh, yes. So very, very angry. All the little children listening got scared. Their parents screamed, pulled their children by the hands and they all ran out of the library."

"Really?"

"Yes, Per. Look at the video."

He showed me his phone video of Konnie reading to the four-year-olds. I watched Konnie read.

"Three little kittens have lost their mittens,
And they began to cry,
'Oh Mother dear, we greatly fear,
Our mittens we have lost ... '
(dramatic pause from Konnie, then:)
'What lost your mittens—ARE YOU FUCKING KIDDING ME?'"

"What does that mean, Per? I don't understand the story. The last part where everyone leaves the library."

"I'm Norwegian, Akito," I babbled, "I don't understand all English words. But I think it's a tradition in English nursery rhymes to make them scary and everyone runs out."

"Ah," said Akito. "Like Halloween or Guy Fawkes. Very scary."

"Guy Fawkes is scary?"

"Oh, yes. Very barbaric. The children burn an image of a real person. Then they throw explosives. It's how you Westerners train terrorists, no?"

"That's in England, Akito. I'm Norwegian."

"Ah."

He put his phone away. "You will not mind if ask Mr. Anglesy from the Tate Modern? About the words that made everyone run from the library? He will know those words, Per. He is English. He will also know about child terrorists."

Mr. Anglesy stood behind us later, while we listened to the coal miner's choir singing. I thought they were good, Mr. Takahashi thought they were good, but Mr. Anglesy murmured "Provincial" to Senor Rossi from the Uffizi gallery.

A little further behind us I saw Iqbal. He was glaring at me. Was he still angry at me over the matter of his four fathers? I ignored him.

Then we went to the town hall where the remaining crafts were on display. Bernie, ever the showman, had decided it was not enough to display things. He had all the artists actively working on their pieces. The Alpaca Mamas were spinning, weaving and knitting next to a display of finished sweaters. Anna Huygens was carefully polishing the newest ceramic layer on her hippo-*cum*-snow goose. Next to the goose, Kristoff's "Tranquility 46" was supported upright by some kind of rickety wooden frame. Kristoff stood in front of it, surrounded by open paint pots, brush in hand, applying another layer of gray paint.

Akito—smartphone recording everything—got into an animated conversation with one of the Alpaca Mamas. There was much bowing and detail about carding wool. Meanwhile, I was drawn irresistibly onward to "Tranquility 46," mainly because Olga was standing there gazing at the painting. I stood behind her marvelling at her exquisite silk and caribou-skin blouse. She would have been gorgeous in rags, but some women have everything. I wondered whether I should greet her, but perhaps we were still on not-speaking terms.

My musings were interrupted by a voice behind me, barely audible in the din of the hall. A single word. "Pig."

I turned. Iqbal, red-faced with anger, was swinging one of Kristoff's big pots of yellow paint at my head.

I ducked. The paint pot hit me a glancing blow, bounced off my head, then hit Olga's back. She staggered into Tranquility 46, and only just managed to keep her balance. Tranquility 46 toppled flat like a redwood under the final cut of a chain saw. I grabbed for the handle of Iqbal's paint pot before he could swing again. Olga was staring at the two of us in mounting anger.

"It wasn't me," I said.

Iqbal let go of the paint, trying to show it wasn't him either. He sidled to the other side of Olga, hoping to leave me holding the paint pot like the guilty idiot.

I was calm. I know how to deal with this kind of situation. There's an approach I have mastered which will rapidly defuse this kind of tense situation. It's childplay, really. What you do is you start by acknowledging the cause of the other person's anger—how the attack was a violation of their person, how their back hurts, or how they have paint on an expensive silk and caribou-skin blouse. Once you have validated their anger, you point out how much you have in common with each other. You point out how you too suffered an unwarranted attack, a glancing blow from Iqbal's paint can, and how you too are covered in paint. Having established common cause, you then look for some action that both of you can take together to improve things. Like blaming Iqbal. It's a very effective process, but you have to take the lead early to control the situation.

Unfortunately, Olga took the lead first.

"I'll teach you to play with paint pots," was all she said. I marvelled at her. Always the lady, not a single curse word. Merely, "I'll teach you." She was magnificent. And her beauty was as hypnotic as ever.

I could not have moved away even if—to take an extreme example and ridiculous example—she were to hit me with a paint pot.

She lifted a big pot of white paint in her left hand and a big pot of green in her right, then she spun twice like an athlete preparing to launch a discus. She let the weight of the paint pots extend her arms ever wider as she whirled. Not a discus thrower now, but an ice dancer, twirling like a flame. I had time to notice again how graceful she was, just before she caught me square on the ribs with one paint pot and simultaneously caught Iqbal square on the head with the other. Her timing and her two-for-one technique were faultless. What a woman! If I had been a judge at an Olympic ice-dancing event, I would have held up a "10" for her. Without hesitation. In spite of the paralyzing pain in my ribs. Iqbal dropped like a shot duck, covered in green paint, straight down onto Tranquility 46.

"Send in the retriever dogs," I thought before the pain from the cracked ribs got me.

I stayed upright for a second longer, hopscotching to keep my balance. I would have succeeded, but for a pot of blue paint, a smaller one. I slid on it and it kicked up from under my foot. I went down too. An evil moment for many reasons. The blue paint pot arced high and came down on the snow goose. Several outer layers of ceramic goose shattered under the impact and fell away. The little blue paint pot remained firmly wedged atop the goose head.

I may have already mentioned how, in times of crisis, my senses speed up and time seems to slow. When I'm in that state of heightened alertness a falling drop of water looks more like a drop of honey reluctantly stretching to detach itself from a spoon. I record every tiny detail in a split second.

I saw Iqbal get shakily to his knees and run for the door, leaving a trail of green paint footprints on Tranquility 46 as he sprinted across the canvas. I saw Kristoff brandish a palette knife at him and shout, "*Ik zal je keel doorsnijden, moederneuker.*"

I noted with detachment that there was not a single "O" sound in this phrase.

I don't speak Dutch, but I understood in that microsecond that "*moeder*" is "mother." Taken together with the threatening knife, I calculated with blinding speed what "*moederneuker*" meant.

I saw Kristoff ran after Iqbal leaving yet another trail of footprints across Tranquility 46, this time in bright yellow. I saw that Anna's goose looked more graceful now that it had shed so many outer layers. I saw Anna was launching herself at me. As time slowed for me, she seemed to hang over me in midair, barely moving towards the apex of the arc that would let her drop down onto me. I saw that she was heavily built and that, when she fell, it would hurt.

I heard her shouting, "O, o, you've broken my bird."

In that same split second my eyes swept the room to Mr. Takahashi. I saw he was holding up his smartphone to video the scene. He was smiling. At least that part of my day, keeping Mr. Takahashi happy, seemed to be going well.

My last view of Olga before Anna landed on me was Olga looking serenely beautiful, in spite of the splashes of paint. Inge once told me women should never combine more than three colours in their outfits. With the various paint splashes Olga had at least seven colours. If anything, they made Olga look even more fashionable and desirable.

Anna landed on me, thrashing her fists and shouting, "O, o, I'll kill you."

Time and pain sped back up to normal speed and abnormal pain.

I tried to tell her about my cracked ribs, but with my head buried under her, I doubt she heard.

Olga grabbed Anna by the hair and threw herself onto us shouting, "No, you won't."

I was cheered by this until Olga continued: "I will."

Then they were pulling at each other shouting.

"O, o, no, me."

"No, me, I'll kill him."

"O no. He's mine."

"MINE."

"O, o, stand in line, bitch."

I wriggled out from under and ran. I could hear them all the way to the exit door.

"Let go my hair."

"You let go *my* hair. O, o, that hurt, you two-faced twat."

"What did you just call me?"

"O ouch, O ouch. You're hurting me."

"Apologize."

"O stop, please stop."

"Not until you apologize."

And so on until I was clear of the town hall.

When I got home, Inge stared at me.

"What happened?"

"I got hit on the head and ribs with a paint pot. Then Olga and Anna fought over me. Your magazines say women have a hard time to achieve Os. Anna managed at least a dozen while they were fighting.

Your magazines are wrong. Is it easier if you're Dutch?"

"Get into the car, Per," said Inge. "You're concussed and delirious. I'm driving you to the hospital to get checked out."

I didn't see Bernie for another week. When I finally caught up with him in The Other Tooth, he was looking surprisingly pleased.

"I thought the Culture Day was a disaster, Bernie?"

"Look at this, Per."

He spread out a magazine called Art Deals International. The centre spread was a picture of Anna's goose. The extraneous layers were mostly missing, shattered by the blue paint pot. The pot was still wedged on the goose's head. In short, it looked exactly the way I'd last seen it.

"Ja, ja, I recognize it." I hung my head in shame.

"Read it, Per."

I read.

> *"The Uffizi gallery has paid three million euros for a stunning work by ceramicist Anna Huygens. The goose was built up with layers of kiln-fired clay, then selectively pared back to its essentials using the ancient Greek excavated-layer technique. At first glance it might be just a graceful snow goose in flight. However, the turban-like blue can on its head; the wide-eyed, shy sideways glance from the bird; and the single splash of sparkling white paint on the lower side of the head, offset against the otherwise muted ceramic, hint at something else. It is nothing other*

than both one of the most subtle satires and one of the most ingenious homages we have ever seen of Vermeer's 'Girl with a Pearl Earring.' Not surprisingly, the Uffizi has dubbed this startlingly beautiful work 'Goose with a Pearl Earring.'

The work was discovered by Uffizi's Senor Ugo Rossi on the Island of Naarlen, an up-and-coming artistic haven."

"That's good, Bernie. Congratulations. Still, Kristoff must be upset at the loss of his painting."

"What loss, Per? Read this."

Bernie flipped open a second magazine. It showed Kristoff's canvas with splashes of spilled paint, Iqbal's footsteps and Kristoff's footsteps. I could see where Olga in her paint-soaked silk and caribou blouse had rolled across the canvas like a human paint brush. The flat part would be the back of her blouse. The parts where the paint was applied only in two perfect circles, there and there, would be the impressions of... I closed my eyes and did deep breathing exercises. The doctors at the hospital had been very clear. I was to avoid all excitement for the next month. I deliberately shut the magazine.

"No, no," said Bernie. He reopened the photo of Kristoff's ruined paining.

"Read this, Per."

I covered the image of the ruined painting with my hand and concentrated religiously only on the text below.

"At an auction in Geneva, the Tate gallery outbid other enthusiasts for Kristoff Huygen's

giant work 'Tranquility 46.' The winning bid was seven million euros. The Tate's senior curator, John Anglesy, said the footprints across the mostly gray canvas are emblematic of man's intrusion into the tranquility of the arctic. The bright colours across the lower left portray the delicate arctic blooms of high summer and provide a perfect visual counterbalance to the stark footprints. Mr. Anglesy says that the work was produced in a tightly controlled piece of performance art which was captured on video and will be displayed alongside this remarkable work."

"Did Mr. Takahashi bid on this, Bernie?"

"He had a lovely visit, Per, he sent me a note thanking you too for his lovely time here. He invites you to visit him in Japan whenever you wish. He will teach you Japanese words to scare children."

"But did he bid on Tranquility 46?"

"I did ask him, Per. He had a great visit, but he didn't think much of Kristoff's painting."

"What did he say, Bernie, when you asked him if he bid on it?"

Bernie pulled out a crumpled letter and scanned it.

"Here it is Per, he says ... wait ... no ... that's not it ... it's near the bottom ... ah, here, he says, 'Are you fucking kidding me?'"

"He wrote that? Exactly that?"

"Yer."

"Ha, ha. What a joker."

"Yer. He always was."

"How do you know him, Bernie?"

"We were in uni together, Per. In Canberra, before we were both asked to leave. He had a reputation even then. Would play the stereotype of the polite Japanese and then suddenly swear like a trooper."

"In English?"

"Of course, in English, Per. It was Australia. He made all the barmaids in Canberra blush with his language. And the barmen too. And he was a terrible prankster. That's why I asked you to escort him. I was scared he'd draw a moustache on Anna's goose, or sign the base as though it was his work, or moon the miners' choir, or scrawl obscenities on Kristoff's painting. You did a great job of keeping him out of trouble. Thank you, Per."

"Nei, nei, that's fine," I said.

"By the way, Per, Kristoff gave Olga a very large share of the money the Tate paid him. In return for Olga's ruined blouse, and for the colour that Olga transferred to the lower left of the painting. Kristoff says that colour, the Arctic blooms, was the crucial missing piece to his painting. Kristoff's very grateful to Olga. He says it's opened up his new vision on how to paint. Human paintbrushes. Tranquility 47. He's very excited."

"Ja, ja, I see, Bernie. Very good."

"Kristoff and Anna are fully sponsoring next year's Naarlen Culture Day Festival. It won't cost Naarlen taxpayers anything. We're an international draw now, you know."

"Ja. You did well, Bernie. Your festival is a hit."

There was a long pause. I didn't want to ask. Bernie guessed.

"You want to know about Olga, Per?"

"Nei, nei, she's an ungrateful shit. I don't care what she thinks."

We were silent again.

Finally, I said, "Ja, ja, OK, why not, Bernie? Go ahead, tell me. Is she talking to me now?"

Bernie looked uncomfortable.

"What do the doctors say about your concussion?"

"I'm fine, Bernie. Just tell me whether Olga and I are on speaking terms now."

"I'm still working on it, Per. Give it time."

"Oh. Why? What does she say?"

"Well, I talked to her about you. She's aware that you would like to be on better terms with her."

I felt hopeful. Akito Takahashi's video had gone viral in Naarlen. Surely by now Olga had seen it. Surely by now she knew that it was Iqbal that had swung the paint pot at her back, not me.

"Ja, Bernie?"

"She said she doesn't deserve you."

"That's sweet, right Bernie?"

"Not really, Per."

"Why not, Bernie?"

"She said, 'I don't deserve him. I must have done something REALLY bad in a previous life. Tell him, next time he comes near me, I'll kill him.'

"Oh."

"Another coffee, Per?"

"No."

"You look tired, Per."

"Ja, ja, the concussion, the ribs. It's been a hard week. I think I'll go home now. To Inge. And Attila."

I went.

*

8. The Tower of Babel

So here we are again in Naarlen, seventy-eight degrees north in the Arctic Ocean. A place that would be empty, icy wilderness except for the lure of palladium, platinum, nickel, coal, a quick buck and a refuge from the law. No surprise that Naarlen attracts miners, claim jumpers, fortune hunters, con artists, lunatics and those on the run from every nation and language group on earth.

The official languages are English and French, but you're just as likely to hear Russian, Spanish, Dutch, Swedish, Norwegian, Danish, German, Amharic, Urdu, Swahili and a dozen more. Which makes Naarlen not only a magnet for society's misfits, it also creates a simmering stew for grudges and vendettas fuelled by nothing more than language misinterpretation.

Every day I have to zig-zag around language pitfalls and potholes. I grew up Norwegian; English nuances defeat me. Take the thousands and one English names for animals.

A dog may be a cur, mutt, mongrel, hound, mastiff, bitch, pup or a pug. But if I call you a dog in English, it's apparently not the same as if I call you a mongrel, mutt, cur or bitch.

Cats can be felines, cats, kittens, queens, toms, tabbies, grimalkins, pussies, pussycats, mousers, moggies, and mogs. I may like cats but, if I call someone catty, this is not good. How logical is that?

Don't even get me started on equines. In English, if I call you an ass, you're an idiot; if I call you a horse's ass, you're an objectionable idiot; if I call you a donkey, you're a stupid idiot; but if I call you a mule, you're a drug runner.

Wait. What? How did that happen? How is anyone supposed to learn this? It's an impossible language for an outsider like me. It's a witches' brew just waiting for someone to get a fist in the face over some perceived difference between ass and mule.

Which brings me to Count and Countess Viktor and Inese Ivanov. They arrived in early spring in a privately chartered jet when the ice was still thick in Naarlen Harbour. Their jet was a long-distance luxury affair, and had travelled direct from Malpensa Airport near Italy's Lago Como. They were the sole passengers.

Customs and immigration controls at our tiny airport are rudimentary. The Ivanovs presented passports from Liechtenstein. Jesus Montanaro, customs and immigrations officer, who is also the Naarlen control tower, baggage handling, duty-free and aviation fuel, squinted at the passports, looked at the colourful permanent residence visas from the Canadian embassy in Liechtenstein, examined their baggage, made sure they had adequate funds deposited at a Canadian bank and let his dog sniff their luggage and visa.

Jesus's dog is a poodle. She's called "Peter" because ... well obviously she's called Peter. Like the original, she is not trained for sniffing drugs or illegal agricultural products. What she can sniff without any training, is food, which she sniffs as enthusiastically as at her last supper. She sniffs, and if the people look anxious, Jesus dives deeper.

Jesus says, "I'm the immigrations officer. She's the psychologist. She reveals people's repressed fears and anxieties. You may call her my assistant, but by civil service career grades, as a psychologist she outranks me. Which is why I have to scoop her poop, and not the other way round. I dream of having an assistant to scoop my poop."

Jesus is odd.

The Ivanov's baggage was food-free except for canned caviar—a whole case. Their Canadian bank deposit, wired ahead from somewhere in Zurich, was the largest that Jesus had ever seen. The other thing that Peter sniffed out was a cat in a carry crate. The Ivanovs had all the veterinary papers ready.

Immigration is a manual paper process at Naarlen airport.

The countess, perhaps weary from her long flight, ogled the paper work and said, "Jesus! How long will this take?"

Jesus has a badge visible on his shirt. It carries his full name. He's still not sure if the countess's comment was first-name friendliness or impatience.

Aside from that one comment, he says, the couple seemed pleasant.

They said they had fallen in love with the Arctic, its people and its scenery during previous visits, and wanted to establish a holiday base here for further travel. Their charter jet, they explained, had come from Lago Como, where they kept a summer villa.

Jesus stamped the entry dates into their passport. The entry stamp has a blank space where the admitting officer must write his or her name. Jesus pulled out a much-chewed pen and wrote "Jesus" in the blank space. He jokes that if ever he forgets how to write his name, he can just make a cross. The teeth marks on the pen are part human, part canine.

Jesus welcomed the new arrivals to Naarlen, then went out onto the runway to refuel the jet for its return to Italy.

The Ivanov's put up in Bernie's new luxury hotel for some weeks and then rented the old Jarlson mansion. It belonged to one of the earliest and richest Palladium miners. The Ivanovs had a bit of work done on it—mainly reflooring and repainting the ballroom-*cum*-dining room. After that, they moved in, cat and all. It seemed they intended to put down roots, at least for a while.

We Naarlanders found them oddly old-world.

The count dressed in immaculate suits and ties, with matching handkerchiefs folded in the suit breast pockets, wore monogrammed shirts with gold cufflinks, and walked with an ebony walking stick. He was somewhat older than the countess, and the more formal of the two.

He would say things like, "We are not in Liechtenstein, so 'My Lord' is not required, but it *is* 'Count Ivanov,' never 'Mr. Ivanov.'"

Then he would smile charmingly to offset the severity of his lecture.

On another occasion, with John Littleham, he was colder. He raised his eyebrows, banged his cane hard on the ground, and said, "Only family uses my first name. Count Ivanov is the correct form of address."

Most of us were fine with that, because John is a creep and a brown-noser who needed to be put in his place.

It was rumoured the count had been an Olympic athlete in his youth with sword or épée or some such, and that he had even fought an illegal duel. Certainly, he looked ready to use his ebony cane to skewer anyone who became overly familiar.

Normally this would have been laughed at, but the Ivanovs somehow got away with it. Naarlanders even began to treasure their odd formality and find it endearing. Perhaps some hidden longing for our own Naarlen royalty had been uncovered. It was as though rubbing shoulders with a count and countess elevated the rest of us from mere hoi polloi, fugitives, dreamers, exiles and no-hopers to people of status too.

The countess dressed as well as her husband, or even better, but said little when in the count's presence other than, "Yes, Viktor," and "No, Viktor."

This, of course, drove the women of Naarlen frantic with curiosity. My wife, Inge, was no exception. That explained the triumphant fashion in which she waved a letter at me over breakfast.

"You'll never guess, Per."

"Probably not, dear."

"Guess."

"Why?"

"Because you'll never guess."

"Inge, why would I guess when you assure me it's futile?"

"That's not the point. Guess."

"What is the point?"

"Don't be a spoilsport, Per. Guess what's in the letter. I'll give you a clue. It's exciting."

"Your friend, Anne from Kirkland Lake, is coming to visit."

A man can dream.

"No. Guess again. It's exciting."

In my younger years I might have said, "Anne coming to stay is exciting," or "dreaming of Anne is exciting," but bitter experience has shown Inge can be very moody about this type of random guessing.

Instead, I merely said, "I give up."

"We've been invited, Per, to a grand dinner to be held by the Count and Countess Ivanov at their Naarlen home for all their new and dear Naarlen acquaintances. Dinner will be catered by Henri and his waitstaff from the Narwhal's Tooth. Dress is formal. RSVPs and any notice of food allergies are appreciated. Isn't that wonderful? I'll have to book an appointment for my hair before the salon is booked out. Do you think, Per, formal means cocktail dress or does it mean evening gown?"

"Yes."

"No," she said, considering my answer, "I don't think so, Per. Not cocktail dress. I think evening gown. Isn't this exciting?"

"Not really, Inge."

"You men. You repress your feelings and your spontaneous joys, Per. You must let them bubble out and share them with me. I'm your wife. Now really, what do you think?"

Again, I could have said that really, a visit from the lovely Anne would be preferable, but I've learned not to take literally these invitations to open the hidden areas of my soul to my wife.

"I look forward to seeing you in your evening gown, dear."

"And you'll wear your tuxedo and cummerbund, Per."

"Yes, dear."

My intuition was ringing alarm bells. My intuition is reliable, only ... only, how can I explain it ...? Imagine, it's ten minutes before noon. Someone hands you a ticking time bomb. You take the bomb and see that it's set to explode at noon. You glance at your watch and see it's running a minute slower than the clock on the time bomb. Eleven minutes to noon.

"Damn," you say, and feel glum. "Look at that. Nei, nei, that's not good, my watch is running slow again. A whole minute. I'm going to have to buy another damn watch battery."

That's my intuition for you. It's reliably correct on feelings of foreboding, but gets the reasons for foreboding spectacularly wrong.

Case in point, the Ivanov dinner: I was right to feel anxious, but I thought it was all about the tux. If only I had known.

The big evening came. The Ivanovs had invited citizens for their wealth or civic standing. The wealthy were represented by couples like Anna and Kristoff Huygens, newly wealthy after selling their pathetic art for millions. The solid citizens were represented by Naarlen's doctors, lawyers, pharmacists, city councillors and the like.

Bernie Halloran, our mayor, was not there, which was odd. Councillor Iqbal Srinivasin was not there either, which I understood. He'd been placed on stress leave ever since the incident at the Naarlen Culture Festival.

I was surprised to see my friend David Panigoniak. He was with a date. Both were dressed in formal eveningwear. I recognized his date as a police constable. David is as fine person as you could wish to meet. I was surprised only because the Ivanovs seemed too class-conscious to invite a police sergeant and a rank-and-file policewoman.

There was a band playing softly inside the ballroom-*cum*-dining room. Couples circulated, chatting, taking glasses of champagne and amuse-gueules from Henri's wait staff.

"O, o, Per, darling," said Anna Huygens and gave me a peck on the cheek. She'd tried to kill me last time I saw her because I broke one of her sculptures. She'd forgiven me since, because the original—before I broke it—was ugly and unsaleable. The broken version was a vast improvement. The Uffizi gallery snapped it up for three million euros.

"Look, Per," she pointed at the wall behind me, "is that an original Picasso? O, o, I think so."

I gazed at the thing she was pointing at. It looked like something a three-year-old had finger-painted after eating too much sugar.

I nodded sagely and continued to circulate.

"Per," said David Panigoniak and shook my hand. "Do you know Claire?"

I shook hands with Policewoman Claire.

"Per helped me with a sea rescue of two boys. He's one of my heroes," he said to Claire.

He was referring to a colossal misunderstanding when he'd rescued the Mafia twins. He still credited me for that.

"Listen, Per," he said, leaning close so not to be overheard by anyone but Claire. "Just a word for you only. I know you can be discreet. We're trying to get fingerprints from something the Ivanovs handle. A glass or whatever. Henri's waitstaff are no help, they only speak Basque or Breton. If you can help with the fingerprints, fine, otherwise please, give the Ivanovs a wide berth. Seriously."

Then he and Claire moved on. I had no idea what "a wide birth" meant. A birth? At their age? Did it mean they were religious and born again? English idioms. I gave up.

I scanned the room for Inge. She'd found Olga Harkonnen and was deep in conversation. Olga, the ungrateful witch, had threatened to strangle me if I approached her, so I kept away.

Count Ivanov pinged on a champagne glass and the hubbub died.

"Friends, Naarlanders, thank you for joining the countess and me tonight. It is a great pleasure to see you all, a chance for us to thank you for the warm Naarlen welcome we've experienced. In a moment we'll go to the dining table. When the countess and I have these dinners at home in Liechtenstein, we have the tradition of breaking up the seating. We'd like to do the same here. Please, choose not to sit next to your spouse tonight, sit with someone you haven't spoken to for some time, or with someone new, so that we can all know each other better. We will rotate places again once or twice between courses and each time, please, let's do the same. So now, let's seat ourselves for dinner."

There was an amused murmur from the guests. I saw that Inge and Olga were going to find seating together. I stood alone, hesitating, an unmoving rock as the outgoing tide of people swept by me towards the dinner table.

"Mr. Pederson, would you do me the honour?"

The countess was standing next to me. She held out her arm. I bowed, took her arm and escorted her to a chair near the head of the table. She patted the empty chair next to her. I sat. The count was sitting on the opposite side of the table and looking at us in a less friendly way than his grand speech had indicated.

The countess must have had a champagne or three before the party began. She leaned close to me, placed a hand on my arm and whispered, "Viktor is prone to jealousy when I flirt. He got into trouble once in an illegal duel with someone he was jealous of, so we'll have to behave impeccably."

"Oh," I said. "Impeccably. Of course, Countess."

She took my hand and squeezed it. "I knew I could count on your discretion. For instance..." and she lowered my hand out of sight below table level, "... For instance, if you must squeeze my hand, it should be out of sight under the table cloth. Like this."

"Nei, nei. I wouldn't want to upset your marriage or your husband, Countess."

"Nonsense," she said, gripping my hand firmly. "A bit of jealousy now and then does wonders for keeping a marriage fresh. You've no idea how ardent Viktor was with me after he fought that illegal duel. And it does a woman a power of good to be fought over. I can't begin to tell you how good it feels. Only a woman could understand, a woman fully in touch with her senses and her body."

"Yes, but my wife ..."

Our conversation was interrupted by the arrival of the first course.

To my relief the countess was monopolized by someone on her far side for the next ten minutes. After the first course, the count rose and asked for the room's attention.

"Tonight's occasion is about new friends."

The countess grabbed for my hand under the table and placed it on her thigh. I tried to withdraw it.

"Shh!" she said sternly to me. "Sit still. Don't fidget."

The count glared at me and began again.

"Tonight's occasion is about new friends. But it can also serve a wider purpose to unite us for a larger good."

The room grew quiet.

"Some of you may know that I'm on the board of a charitable fund in Liechtenstein. The fund has turned its attention to combatting global warming and preserving polar bear and cetacean life in the Arctic. A worthwhile cause you'll agree. It's part of the reason I'm here. I'm very proud to announce that our friends Anna and Kristoff Huygens... Would they please join me up here? ... Ah, thank you. I'm pleased to announce that Anna and Kristoff Huygens have written a cheque to the foundation for ... well I won't mention the amount ... but Anna, Kris may I mention seven figures? ... Yes? ... Thank you. I'm overwhelmed by their good will, so much so that the countess and I will match their donation."

The guests around me banged on the table enthusiastically and applauded. The countess inched my hand higher on her thigh.

"Don't be impatient," she whispered and pushed my hand fractionally lower again.

"I should applaud the count," I said. "Perhaps, if I could have my hand...?"

The count glared at my delayed applause.

"This is first and foremost a friendly dinner," he said, "but I will speak to each of you during the evening to see if you would like to support this cause that is close to all our hearts. If you do, I promise you the countess and I will match each and every donation you care to make. And, of course, everyone who joins cause with us becomes family and has a standing invitation to our modest homes in Liechtenstein and in Lago Como, whenever you next find yourself in Europe."

There was a murmur of eager anticipation from the guests. They quieted and the count continued.

“Now please change seating, sit next to someone you don’t know.”

“Not you,” said the countess to me. “You stay here.”

The count stayed where he was too and glared at me. I saw David Panigoniak looking at me with a worried expression. With the arrival of the food, the countess had to relinquish my hand. She picked up a knife and fork and turned to greet her new far-side seating partner. I considered getting up and asking Inge whether we could leave now.

Two problems.

Inge would say, “We’re barely here five minutes and you can’t bear to stay? You do this every time we’re invited out. What is wrong with you, Per?”

Also, Inge was with Olga and I dared not approach. I didn’t know what the countess was up to, but Olga would kill me for certain. Being with the countess was safer. I picked up my utensils and ate. I was enjoying the meal less and less.

Fortunately, when the plates were removed a distraction presented itself. The Ivanov cat appeared from under the table and climbed onto the countess’s lap. It was a large, fluffy cat. A regal-looking longhair.

The countess shifted her chair back slightly. She saw me looking at the animal.

“You like cats, Mr. Pederson? Pat her, please. She’s very friendly.”

The animal looked at me. I looked at it. It rolled onto its back, still on the countess’s lap, but obviously inviting a response from me. I’ve always considered it polite to make a fuss over my host’s pets.

"Excuse me, Countess," I said and leaned forward. The Countess leaned back in her chair to make space. I buried my face on the cat's stomach and blew raspberries. The thing purred quietly and waggled its paws in the air.

"Inese!"

It was the count's voice and he sounded furious. I straightened up. As my head and eyes emerged above table-level, I saw that he was indeed furious. Could it be he wasn't aware of the cat?

The countess seemed distressed and tongue-tied as though she'd been caught doing something wrong. Like a little girl who's been caught with her hand in the cookie jar.

"I'm sorry Viktor," she whispered.

"You promised me never to ... never to ... you said you would control your ... have you no shame...?"

He was hissing at her in a half whisper trying to keep his disagreement with her private.

"I'm truly sorry, Viktor. I don't know what came over me..."

What on earth did she mean? He was getting even more wound up by her apologies. His hands were trembling. He grabbed at a glass of red wine and sipped hastily. Clearly it was to steady his hands and himself. I saw his knuckles were white on the glass.

This was puzzling. No doubt the table was blocking the cat from his view. I needed to defuse whatever the misunderstanding was.

"What a magnificent pussy," I said in my most polite guest tones.

"Gaaagh." The count made a choking noise and two jets of red wine shot from his nostrils.

"I demand satisfaction," said the count and shot up.

He was quivering with rage while blotting wine from his face and chest. The cat meanwhile, had slid off the countess's lap and disappeared under the table.

The din of conversation around us hid our words from the nearby guests. In any case they were too busy talking and drinking.

"Oh, no, Viktor. Not again," said the countess.

For all her words, she seemed strangely pleased by whatever "I demand satisfaction" meant.

I groped for understanding of this elusive phrase.

"I suppose it's a natural human yearning," I replied.

"We are better than animals! We control our yearnings," he hissed, "but I will not discuss this in front of guests. Come! Both of you."

"Must I, Viktor?"

"You must."

He murmured some brief excuse to those sitting near him and the three of us strode out. To be precise, he strode; the countess followed like a guilty schoolgirl, and I followed in confusion. We descended into the basement of the house. The Ivanovs had converted it into some kind of gym or exercise room.

"What do you know about fencing, Pederson?"

"Well, Ivanov," I said leaving out his title in a tit-for-tat, "I know a bit about it."

It was true. My neighbour, Francesco, had just put up some double strand diamond mesh on the border between our backyards to keep his hens from getting into our garden.

"Good," he said grimly.

He took a sword from a rack on the wall. Not a sabre. It was one of those thin pointy things that swish and flex. A foil. *Herregud*, it suddenly dawned on me what kind of fencing he meant. And these were for real, there were no safety buttons on the pointy ends.

His foil was monogrammed.

"Take your choice," he said. "Any one of the others."

"Do you have to, Viktor?" said the countess. "What if he apologizes, on his knees?"

"For what?" I said, more puzzled than ever.

"Shameless!" said the count. He actually ground his teeth. "And you, Inese, will witness that he insisted on the duel. And I was forced to respond in self-defence."

"Yes, Viktor," she said. Her tone was submissive but there was a flush of excitement on her cheeks.

"Good. Raise your foil, Pederson. Point it to the ceiling like so. This is the traditional salute before we begin. Now begin."

He lowered the point of his sword to my chest level and slashed horizontally. A tear appeared across my tux lapels.

I had not moved. I don't think the count understood why. My feet were rooted. I would have screamed but my voice was gone. I still pointed my foil at the ceiling. My arm seemed as paralyzed as my feet.

I was about to die. "Goodbye Inge," I thought and looked down piously. "And goodbye Olga and Anne from Kirkland Lake."

The count frowned. "You're a cool one, I'll give you that."

A new voice spoke.

"The coolest one on Naarlen."

I knew that voice. David Panigoniak.

I looked up. David was putting handcuffs on the count. Claire was cuffing the countess.

"Thank you, Per. You took a big risk in fencing with him."

"Did I?"

"Bigger than you know. He cheats."

"How?"

"He's done this before. We have the complete modus operandi from Interpol. His sword tip has a toxin. If you hadn't swayed back as he slashed at you, you'd be lying on the floor semi-paralyzed by now. I can tell you my heart was in my mouth as I watched you playing at Mr. Cool."

"*Herregud*," I said. Mr. Cool? The things David didn't know.

"He didn't scratch you, did he?"

I looked frantically at my chest. My shirt was whole.

"Nei, nei. No scratch."

"That's not all. His foil is a working foil. Yours isn't."

"What's not working, David?"

"If you make any sudden movement with your foil, the blade will fall from the handle. Just drop off. You'll be defenceless."

"Really?"

"Really, Per. Try."

My blade was still pointed at the ceiling. I angled it further backwards, like a tennis player about to deliver an overhand smash. Then I whipped it forward. If David was right, the motion should detach the blade and drop it onto the floor. It didn't drop. It detached and shot forward like a guided missile, pointed end first. It struck Ivanov in the shoulder. He dropped to the ground whimpering with the blade still firmly planted in him. The handle was still in my hand.

"*Herregud*," I said again, weakly, and, "*Knull meg.*"

"Ambulance please, Claire," said Panigoniak.

She shook her head. "When have those bastards ever co-operated with a police request?"

"Per," said David, "could you phone for an ambulance please? Don't mention police. Claire, can you take the woman into custody."

I fished out my phone and called 666.

The countess was in shock, she said not a word as Claire led her away. I don't think she had known that her husband cheated. The next conversation they had would be ... interesting.

David was staring at the two red streaks on the count's chest. Then he stared at me.

"Amazing," he said. "He's an Olympic fencer. One of the best. And you have a defective foil. And you still managed to get two hits on his chest. You are amazing, Per."

I would have explained that the marks on the Count's shirt were streams of red wine from the count's nose, not blood, but just then two constables appeared, then the paramedics. They took the count away on a gurney.

David and I followed them. The count and countess were carried and led out through the ball room. The conversation ground to a halt. The guests looked at the sword blade sticking up from the count's shoulder, the additional twin streams of "blood" on his chest, and at the sword handle in my hand. A murmur of anger built. Directed at me.

David held up his hand for quiet.

"Ladies, Gents," he said when he had their attention. "The two people you know as Count and

Countess Ivanov are in fact Louis and Olivia Van Zyl. They are not from Liechtenstein. They have no house in Lago Como. They are two dangerous confidence tricksters from Belgium. They are wanted across Europe and by Interpol on several charges. Naarlen police needed to obtain their fingerprints tonight to confirm this. We were able to obtain a wine glass from each thanks to Mr. Pederson who, at great risk to himself, distracted both Van Zyls away from the dining table. The fingerprints on those wine glasses are those of the Van Zyls. Their modus operandi is to appear as rich aristocrats raising funds for a charity. The funds, of course, go into their own pockets, after which the Van Zyls disappear. Thanks to Mr. Pederson's swift intervention, those of you who already donated to the Van Zyls will get your money back."

"Why are they in Naarlen?" shouted someone.

David half turned towards the speaker. "We believe they came to Naarlen after the Huygens sold their works of art for a combined ten million euros. Naarlen became a worthwhile target at that point. Along with news that Mayor Halloran built a luxury hotel."

"How did Per distract them?" shouted someone else.

"Is the count dead?" and "Did Per kill him?" shouted others.

David held up his hand again. "The count is not seriously wounded. I won't comment on the details of Per's distraction until the extradition hearing is completed. For tonight I suggest you continue with your meal. The Van Zyls have paid for a splendid dinner from Henri and The Narwhal's Tooth. The wine is good and the band is playing. Why let an evening among friends go to waste."

"Hear, hear," shouted a few and amidst a huge buzz of talk the diners returned to the table.

"I get the confidence trick," I said to David, but I don't understand the thing with the woman and the swords. What does that have to do with anything?"

David shook his head. "That was the dangerous side of the Van Zyls. Again, we know this from Interpol. Louis Van Zyl was in it for the money. His wife, Olivia, got her thrills another way. She loved to flirt in front of Louis until he started a fight or a duel with whomever she was flirting. She's a sick woman. They're both sick. He enjoyed his role in her ritual. They're a very dangerous pair. Which is why I hoped you'd give them a wide berth."

He paused and studied me. "I should have known if there was danger anywhere, you'd be right into it. How on earth did you persuade her to let you sit with her?"

"Oh, just psychology, you know, David," I said airily. I leaned against a sideboard. It may have given an impression of nonchalance and elegance. The real reason was my knees were like rubber. The sideboard kept me upright.

"You needed help, and I tried to help out," I continued. "Charmed her to invite me to sit with her. How did you get a fingerprint match so quickly?"

"Fingerprint powder on the wine glasses, a cell phone image, and Interpol standing by to receive the image."

"And what tipped you off that they were imposters, David?"

"The visas in their passports were faked. Very good fakes, but still fakes."

"Jesus Montanaro noticed?"

"Not Jesus. Peter. His poodle. She spent too much time sniffing the visas. The forgers had used a plant-based ink for the visas. Apparently, an ink that smells unusually good if you're a poodle. Jesus noticed and tipped us off. It took us a while afterwards to figure out who the imposters might be."

"Couldn't you just demand they give you fingerprints? Instead of secretly trying to get a glass or a plate?"

"No, Per. We needed better grounds than Jesus's poodle. We did check with the Canadian embassy in Liechtenstein, but they were too slow. The Van Zyl's would be long gone with all the Naarlen donations by the time we got their answer."

"Ah."

"Well, you're the hero of the night, Per."

David is one of the most generous souls I know.

"Not to mention, Jesus, Peter, you and your date. I liked your date, David."

"Claire?"

"Ja, ja, Claire."

"Just a colleague, Per," he said, a touch too defensively.

"Too bad, David."

We scanned the diners idly. I saw Inge was again seated with Olga.

"You liked Claire, did you, Per?"

"Ja, ja, David. You made a very handsome couple. I saw you dance together in the ballroom. Too bad that was just duty. She's a great-looking woman, seems nice too. And smart."

He smiled. I thought he'd say more about Claire. All he said was, "Well, I must get back to the station. Thank you for your help."

"Night, David."

He left.

I got within shouting distance of Inge and Olga and waved to Inge.

"Come on over here," shouted Inge and waved me to come over.

"No," I said.

"Olga won't kill you," shouted Inge.

"Yes, she will," I said.

"Yes, I will," shouted Olga.

"Her bark is worse than her bite," said Inge.

"No, it's not," said Olga.

Another ridiculous English idiom to befuddle me. I know a barque is a three masted sailing ship. Every Norwegian child knows that. A bight is a loop of rope or the curve in a bay. But how is that worse than a barque? I tried it in Norwegian.

En bark er verre enn en bukt.

It still made no sense. Olga used to own a fishing fleet, but none of them were sailing ships. Whatever.

"Not coming closer," I shouted.

Inge got up and walked over to me.

"What, Per?"

"Hell of an evening. We should go home."

"No, we're not going. We're barely here five minutes and you can't bear to stay? You do this every time we're invited out. What is wrong with you, Per?"

"Look at my tuxedo."

I thought that would allow us to go home. No such luck.

"Honestly, Per! How on earth do you do such things? It's ruined. You did this deliberately to make sure we could leave, didn't you?"

"No, I..."

"Well, how DID it happen?"

"It's complicated. I..."

"Tell me later. I'm in the middle of something with Olga."

She went back to her seat with Olga. I considered my options and wandered over to The Other Tooth for a coffee.

Edna was working on a beer. She eyed me blearily.

"Well, lookee here. Nice monkey suit. Where's the organ grinder?"

I ignored this.

"What does it mean, Edna, when someone says, 'her barque is worse than her bight'?"

Edna showed her teeth to me, growled aggressively and yipped like a dog.

I backed away. "You should stay away from the hard stuff, Edna. Stick to beer."

"Coffee for you?" asked Bernie.

I sat at the bar and nodded. He passed over the coffee.

"You're not at the big do tonight, then Bernie?"

"Can't stand people who give themselves airs. Very un-Australian. 'Sides which, I had them pegged for con artists the moment they set foot in my hotel lobby. Made them pay in advance with a deposit against room damages, and they weren't happy about it. Tried to stand on their titles and dignity. Told 'em if they didn't like it, they could stand on their titles and dignity outside in the cold."

"You heard what happened tonight?"

"Yer. What did you think of Claire?"

There's a reason Bernie is our mayor. He knows everything that happens in Naarlen.

"Seems like a nice lady. Might be a good match for Panigoniak."

"You did well, Per, but no one will thank you for it."

"Why, Bernie?"

"People had dreams of being invited to swill champagne with nobility. On the shores of Lago Como. They would have been the envy of their neighbours and grandchildren. You popped that bubble. Ruined their dreams."

"Wasn't me, Bernie."

"The way they see it, it was. Worse, they were gullible. That's embarrassing. You weren't gullible. That's annoying. Makes them feel inferior. They'll hate you for this, Per."

"Even the ones who were going to lose money?"

"Especially those, Per."

I sipped my coffee morosely and eyed Bernie.

He shook his head. "Don't ask, Per. I don't know whether Olga had already donated. I doubt it, because she's canny, but I don't know. You'd have to ask Inge to ask Olga."

"Then Inge would want to know why I want to know."

"That's for sure, Per."

"So, I'll never know."

"Probably not, Per. Want something stronger than coffee?"

"No. Just another coffee, but with extra sugar."

"Here. On the house. For unappreciated service to Naarlen."

My premonition machine had quietened down, there was no more forecast of doom, The Tooth and its inhabitants weren't putting on airs; Edna was as grumpy as she always is before beer number three; my ripped jacket fitted in just fine; no one was trying to flirt under the table, and no one wanted to skewer me with a sword. The evening finally felt normal.

"Skol, Bernie."

"Cheers, Per."

*

9. A Cat on a Cold Tin Roof

Naarlen is seventy-eight degrees north. You'd think that the Arctic geography and weather would be at the root of my troubles. Or even the polar bears. Not so.

Sixty percent of my troubles are caused by women.

Think of Grandma Mac getting me taken hostage; or Edna getting me arrested (and puking on me), or Sheilagh Smith nearly getting me drowned.

Another sixty percent of my troubles are caused by cats and dogs.

Nei, nei, don't tell me that adds up to more than a hundred. It adds up to only ninety-five percent of my troubles. There's an overlap; obviously, some of my troubles are caused by both: women with cats or women with dogs or women with both.

Take the thing with Countess Ivanov AND her cat: woman AND cat almost getting me killed in a stupid sword fight.

Or take Klaas van Vuuren. You recall the only reason I agreed to write the Aunt Maude agony column for Klaas's newspaper was because Inge, my wife, wanted a cat.

There you have it again: woman AND cat in one. And look what happened. Inge got her cat, Attila, and the offices of the Naarlen Herald ("Our Community's Voice in the Arctic") burnt down after almost two hundred years in business.

I'd normally be modest, but I have to point out that I was the hero of that event. I rescued Klaas just before the burning building collapsed. It didn't end well for Klaas, though, the poor *gubbe* as we say in Norwegian. The insurance company refused to pay out. Police and medics all testified that Klaas fought against his rescue, beat at me with his fists and swore he would kill me. Then he sang "Happy Birthday" in the ambulance.

The insurance company said Klaas set the fire deliberately to kill himself. They reached a stand-off with Klaas: as long as Klaas doesn't take the insurance company to court for not paying out, they won't sue him for arson.

Klaas reached a stand-off with the police too. They won't prosecute for arson as long as he gets counselling for his problems. Of course, part of his imagined problems were me, so I wasn't entirely surprised when Klaas's psychologist, Paul Allan, phoned me.

"Hey Paul."

"Hey Per. Klaas's counselling with me is progressing well. Can you drop by for tomorrow's counselling session? I need to see that he can react well to your presence. Unexpected presence."

"Oh."

"Don't worry, Per. It will be fine."

"Umm, Paul? Last time I saw him, he swore he'd kill me."

"He's much better now, Per. I've been doing hypnosis sessions with him to get rid of his paranoia, make him more positive about what he can achieve against adversity and with the help of friends. Also, for tomorrow, I've hired Edna in the unlikely event we need some extra muscle to restrain him."

"Oh."

Edna—my sometimes nemesis—is built like a stone blockhouse and is pure muscle.

"Don't be nervous, Per. You rescued him from the fire. Take the next step to help me heal his mind."

"Very well, Paul. I suppose."

"Thanks, Per. See you tomorrow at 2 p.m. then in my office."

"Hello, Klaas," I said when I walked in.

Klaas turned white.

"You!" he said. He seemed to have difficulty breathing.

"Hello, Klaas. Paul asked me to come today."

"Yes, Klaas," said Paul. "You remember we talked about doing this someday? We've visualized this moment and practised for it. Time to see whether you can react calmly. I trust you. You can do it. Breathe deeply and count to three."

"Godverdomme tyfushoer!" Klaas shouted at me and picked up a chair to throw.

It didn't look or sound very calm. Can *"Godverdomme tyfushoer"* really be how you count to three in Dutch?

Klaas flung the chair at me, swore when it missed, then flung himself at me. Edna caught Klaas in the middle of his leap at me, as easily as one of those cricket players stretching out a lazy gloved hand to snap a ball out of the air. While Edna held Klaas, Paul played soothing music and spoke to Klaas calmly.

When that didn't work, Edna sat on Klaas for the remainder of the session.

You wouldn't want Edna leaning on you, never mind sitting on you.

"We'll try again in a few weeks, Per," said Paul. "Klaas is progressing nicely. That went not too badly. Thank you for dropping in. I will now do some positive-suggestion hypnosis for him. And he and I will have some Dutch spekulaas cookies. They're very calming."

It was a long road, but with persistent help from Paul, Edna and yours truly, Klaas slowly learned to greet me with genuine friendliness every time we saw each other in Paul's offices. It looked to me similar to training a dog. Instead of dog treats he got Dutch cookies when he smiled on command.

I remember the breakthrough day that Klaas stood up and shook hands with all of us. It was quite touching. I think a few of us had to wipe away a furtive tear.

"Ja, nee," Klaas said. "I see it all now. I don't know why it took me so long. I set the fire myself. I can't tell you why. I was a different person then. Perhaps it was because Trudie had left me for some man in Vietnam. But now, I'm cured. Thank you, Paul. I have new-found confidence. I feel close to invincible. Thank you, Edna. And above all, thank you Per. You were very brave to rescue me from the fire. I'm glad I'm well enough to finally thank you properly."

At the end of that session, Klaas and I left Paul's office together. Klaas was headed home, and my path took me past his home.

"Come," I said to him, "we'll walk together."

At Klaas's house, he stopped in surprise. He pointed to the roof. There was a cat on the roof, peering down on us. It looked anxious, trapped.

I should have remembered the fifty percent of my troubles start with cats. It was the absence of women that made me miss that clue.

"That's my cat, Saartje, Per. How did she get up there?"

"Perhaps she climbed that telephone pole—that one over there—and then jumped across, Klaas?"

"Ja, nee," he said. "But how do I get her down?"

"Do you have a ladder and a basket?"

"Ja, a ladder, ja, and a small basket."

"Climb the ladder, get the cat, put her in the basket."

"I can't climb down while also holding the basket, Per."

"You put the cat in the basket, I'll climb the ladder high enough so that you can reach down from the roof and hand me both."

"Oh, that's good. You're a good friend, Per. I'm sorry I was so mean to you. When I was sick."

"Nei, nei, that's all behind us. Go get the basket."

I know you're anticipating some kind of disaster story, but the cat rescue went like clockwork.

Saartje, the cat, sat calmly in the basket. I climbed part way up the ladder. Klaas lay flat on the roof and stretched one arm down to where I could take the cat and basket from him. Easy.

Once the cat and I were off the ladder, Klaas turned his bum towards the ladder and felt for the top rung with a toe.

The thing with keeping clocks and clockworks running smoothly, is you have to remember to rewind them.

"Oops."

"Careful, Klaas."

His foot knocked the ladder sideways. It fell and landed badly. The top three rungs cracked against a rock. I held my breath. Fortunately, Klaas hadn't committed his weight to the ladder. He was still safely on the roof.

"You OK, Klaas?"

"Ja, OK, Per. No problem. Can you put the ladder back?"

"Actually, there is a problem, Klaas, the top end is broken it won't reach quite high enough."

"Oh. That's not good, Per."

"Nei, nei. Not great. Still, no one is hurt and we got your cat down."

"What about me, Per? How do I get down?"

"I'll call the fire department. They have ladders."

"Good idea."

I dialled 555. Naarlen has its own emergency numbers. 555 is for fire unless you're French-speaking. Don't ask.

I got through to the fire chief, Amandi Musa.

Amandi has grown cynical after years of firefighting. He doesn't believe any fire is an accident. Ever. Not a single one. In his book all fires are caused by idiots.

"You left the frying pan on the stove unattended while you answered the phone and had a long chat with your mother? And guess what, the oil in the pan went up in flames? That's no accident, that's negligence and a predictable fire. You're an idiot.

"The fuel gauge on your car doesn't work? You used a candle to check the level in your gas tank and the tank exploded? That's no accident, that's stupidity and a predictable fire. You're an idiot.

"You ran an overloaded electric extension cable under a carpet and it set the carpet alight? Gross negligence with a predictable outcome. No accident. You're simply an idiot."

He says in Nigeria, the part that he comes from, they love to bargain, which may also explain some of what happened next.

Me: "Hi Amandi, it's Per Pederson."

Amandi: "Per, my friend, how nice. How are you?"

Me: "Good Amandi, how are you and the family?"

Amandi: "Good, although my mother-in-law and her hangers-on are still with us."

Klaas (shouting): "Are they coming?"

Me to Klaas: "No, they're still visiting with Amandi. And you don't want them."

Me to Amandi: "Ei, ei, that's not good."

Klaas: "What's not good?"

Amandi: "These things are sent to try us, Per."

Me: "I thought judges were sent to try us, Amandi."

Amandi: "Geh, geh, geh. Good one. So, what's up, Per? Has some idiot started a fire?"

Me: "No, some idiot is stuck on the roof of his house. Can you bring a truck with a ladder?"

Klaas: "I'm not an idiot."

Me to Klaas: "Nei, nei. It's just how Amandi talks. Everyone's an idiot."

Amandi: "Who's the idiot on the roof?"

Me to Amandi: "Klaas van Vuuren. Can you bring a ladder?"

Klaas: "Maybe Amandi's the idiot."

Amandi: "Did he just say I was the idiot?"

Me to Amandi: "Come Amandi, we're amongst friends. No one's an idiot."

Amandi: "So if he's not an idiot, how come he's stuck on a roof? Geh, geh, geh, geh."

Klaas: "What does he say?"

Me to Klaas: "Says if you're not an idiot, how come you're ... look never mind, Klaas, it's just the way he likes to joke."

Klaas: "Stop joking and tell the idiot to bring a ladder."

Amandi: "I heard that."

Me to Amandi: "Can you bring a ladder?"

Amandi: "Is there a fire?"

Me to Amandi: "No."

Amandi: "Listen, Per, my friend. Fire department can only come for two reasons. One: fire. Two: animal stuck in a high place. We don't do people stuck in high places. Not birds either, and not snakes or crocodiles."

Me to Amandi: "Snakes and crocodiles on roofs? You get those?"

Amandi: "In Africa. Snakes a plenty. Crocodiles only once, in a tree after a flood, and it was a small one. But the owner of the tree said he couldn't pick his mangos, what with the crocodile stuck up there."

Me to Amandi: "What did you do?"

Amandi: "Told him what I just told you. We don't do crocodiles. Nor gators, nor monitor lizards, nor komodo dragons."

Me to Amandi: "Oh. Well, no dangerous animals today. Klaas and I just got his cat off the roof. That's why he's up there. Now his ladder is broken. I mean after we got the cat down and before we got Klaas down."

Amandi: "Well, don't put the cat back up there. We do cats on roofs, but not when people put them back."

Klaas: "What does Amandi say?"

Me to Klaas: “Says no. Won’t come unless there’s a fire.”

Klaas: “So what should we do, Per?”

Me to Klaas: “Offer a donation to the Fire Department.”

Klaas: “Would that change his mind?”

Me to Amandi: “Amandi, Klaas would like to make a donation to the Fire Department. Do you think you could send a man around to collect his donation? I mean a man with a ladder so that Klaas can come down and make a donation?”

Amandi: “Very expensive, Per, to send a ladder truck around just to collect a donation. How big a donation?”

Me to Klaas: “Yes. If the donation is generous.”

Klaas: “Ask him how much.”

Me to Amandi: “Amandi, how generous a donation?”

Amandi: “Is he an idiot or someone important?”

Me to Klaas: “He wants to know if you’re an idiot or someone important. Admit to being an idiot. It’s cheaper.”

Klaas: “What ‘admit?’”

Me to Klaas: “I mean just pretend you’re an idiot, it will be cheaper.”

Klaas: “No. Important. Editor Emeritus of the Naarlen Herald.”

Me to Amandi: “He says he’s important.”

Amandi: “Sixty dollars. Any less would be an insult to an important person.”

Me to Klaas: “Sixty dollars.”

Klaas: “Tell him thirty.”

Amandi to me: “I heard. Tell him he’s an idiot and it’s seventy-five dollars.”

Me to Klaas: “He says seventy-five.”

Klaas: “Does he take me for an idiot? Twenty-five dollars and not a cent more. My last offer.”

Amandi: “Yes, I take him for an idiot. Eighty dollars and not a cent less.”

Me to Klaas: “Eighty dollars. Not a cent less. Klaas, you really should say, ‘yes.’”

Klaas (proudly): “Per, you mean well. In the old days I might have said, ‘yes.’ Nowadays, never. Paul Allen has given me new-found confidence in my ability to overcome adversity. Especially with friends like you by my side. Tell him what he can do with himself. You can tell him in good Dutch from me, ‘*Ga neuk jezelf.*’”

Me to Amandi: “Hey Amandi... Amandi?”

Me to Klaas: “He hung up.”

Klaas looked down. “Do you think I could jump down, Per?”

“Nei, nei, you mustn’t jump Klaas. I know Paul’s hypnosis makes you feel invincible, but jumping, nei, nei, you’ll kill yourself.”

“What should I do?”

“Do your neighbours have ladders, Klaas?”

“No. And they don’t speak to me. I once told them the same thing I just suggested for Amandi.”

“Oh. Maybe I should call Paul?”

“Paul Allen?”

“Yes.”

“OK, Per.”

I called. “Hello, Paul. It’s Per Pederson. Klaas is on the roof of his house.”

“Oh Lord. Does he want to jump, Per?”

“I’ve told him not to.”

“Can you keep him calm until I get there?”

“Do you have a ladder, Paul?”

“No.”

"Never mind then, Paul."

I hung up.

Klaas was waving to me.

"Never mind about Paul, Per. I have an idea."

"What idea, Klaas?"

"You'll see. It's brilliant. Can you go to the corner store? It's just down the road, thirty seconds walk, get me a dozen newspapers, a lighter and a big can of barbecue firestarter—the liquid type. I'll pay you back."

"Ja, but for what, Klaas."

"You remember what the fire department said? They'll come if there's a fire. I'm going to start a small fire."

"You can do that safely?"

"Ja, nee, no problem, Per."

I walked to the corner store. The defunct Naarlen Herald had been replaced by a new paper, a tabloid called the Naarlen Enquirer. The headline that day read:

"Salman Rushdie and Elvis—Did Both have a Naarlen Safe House?"

"Twelve copies please," I said to the kid behind the counter.

"Twelve, Mr. Pederson? No one has ever bought twelve. Do you have some connection with the Salman Rushdie story? I'm a big fan of 'Midnight's Children.'"

"Is that an Elvis song?"

"No, Mr. Pederson. I don't know who Elvis is. 'Midnight's Children' is a Salman Rushdie book."

He looked carefully at the Naarlen Enquirer photos of Elvis and Salman and squinted at my face.

"Do I look like either one?"

"No-o-o, Mr. Pederson, but you could have had plastic surgery. I sell photos to the Naarlen Enquirer as a sideline. Could I take your photo?"

He took my photo and said, "If you are Salman, I'm a big fan of your books, but not of your lifestyle. So many marriages. That's not a good thing. Sorry, I have to be honest. I hope you'll stick with your current wife."

"Inge. She'd kill me if I didn't."

"Inge? Is there a new one already? I hoped you'd stick with Padma. How do you do it?"

"Whatever."

I paid for the papers, the lighter, the big can of firestarter and returned to Klaas.

"I've got it worked out, Per. Put all that in the little basket. Right. Now put the ladder back. I know it's broken... There... Now climb the ladder as high as you can ... before the broken part ... and hand me the basket. If we both stretch ... you should be able to ... even on the broken ladder... there, I have the basket."

"OK, Klaas. Now what? I can't see what you're doing up there."

"I'm using my brains, Per. And my new-found confidence from Paul Allen. I'm wedging the basket into the top of the chimney. It's all brick and concrete. Perfect fire barrier. So ... the basket fits, nicely. Now I pour firestarter on the newspapers ... so ... thorough soaking of firestarter ... that's a big can of firestarter soaking the basket..."

"Klaas... Klaas, are you sure about this ... it sounds kind of..."

"Nee, nee, don't worry my friend. I've got this."
There was a "WOOF" as he applied the lighter to the basket of firestarter-soaked newsprint.
"Is it working, Klaas?"
"It's burning. Not much smoke, but definitely burning. Very hot. You think I should call the fire department now, Per? Or wait for smoke?"
"Call them now, Klaas."
I could see him fiddle with his phone. It was odd, there was no smoke from the top of the chimney, but looking through the front window of his house, it seemed darker in there than before. Was that smoke INSIDE the house?
"Per, my cell phone battery has died. Can you call?"
"OK, Klaas."
I called and got through to Amandi again.
"Hello Amandi."
"Per, has the idiot on the roof changed his mind about the ninety dollars?"
"Actually, Amandi, he's got a real fire now ... '
"Per, do you know what my name, Amandi, means in the Igbo language?'
"No, Amandi. What?"
"It means 'Trust no one.' So, don't kid me Per. There's no fire, he's just trying to get out of paying."
I looked again at the front window. Klaas's living room furniture, still visible a moment ago was now obscured by thick black smoke. And those little moving bright spots, were those flames?
"No really, Amandi, it's..."
"Per, call me back when he's willing to pay. Ninety-nine dollars and ninety-nine cents. A bargain. Not a cent less."
He hung up.

"Klaas," I shouted, "what's in your fireplace?"

"Oh," he shouted back. "I never use that. I keep books and boxes, gift wrapping paper and decorations left over from Christmas."

"I think your firestarter poured down the chimney and set that alight."

"You mean, a real fire, Per?"

"Yes."

"*Ooo, lieve hemel, nu zit de stront in de kut!* Is the fire department coming, Per?"

"No. They think you're kidding. Amandi's name in Nigeria translates into 'trust no one.'"

"Fok. That is not good, Per."

"Nei."

"I didn't think all those newspapers would let the firestarter leak through. What do we do? Should I jump?"

A man had parked his car near us and was climbing out.

"Not yet, Klaas. I'll ask this gentleman to call the firefighters. They may believe him."

"Can you call the fire department?" I shouted.

"What fire?" he said.

Just then, the front window of Klaas's house blew out from the heat of the fire inside.

The newcomer eyed the black smoke billowing out and grabbed his cell phone. He was brief.

"On their way," he shouted back. He walked over.

"Hank Diefenbaker," he said, sticking out a hand to me.

I shook. "Per Pederson."

"How did the fire start, Mr. Pederson?"

"Klaas poured firestarter down the chimney and lit it."

"That's Klaas van Vuuren up there on the roof then, is it, Mr. Pederson?"

"Yes."

"And the big gallon tin in his hand, that's the jug of firestarter he used?"

"Yes."

Klaas was shouting down from the roof. "Who is it, Per?"

"It's someone called Hank Diefenbaker. Seems he knows you. And don't jump, fire department is coming."

"Oh, Diefenbaker. Ja. He's from my insurance company. We're supposed to sign mutual release forms for my office fire. You know the one, the fire at the Naarlen Herald."

"Can't sign them now, van Vuuren," shouted Diefenbaker.

"What?"

Klaas leaned over the edge of the roof to hear better. Diefenbaker climbed part way up the ladder.

I grabbed the ladder to steady it.

Paul Allen appeared next to me. I hadn't heard his car arrive.

"It's OK Klaas," he shouted. "Everything is fine. Don't jump."

The smoke was getting thicker. We were all coughing.

"What did you say, Diefenbaker?" coughed Klaas.

"Said we won't sign the ... cough ... release forms with you, van Vuuren."

There was a flash of bright light. The kid from the corner store, the part-time photographer for the Naarlen Enquirer, was photographing the scene.

"Is this the Elvis-Rushdie safe house?" he asked me. "Is it an assassination attempt?"

"Why no ... cough ... release forms, Diefenbaker?" shouted Klaas from the roof.

"Arson again, van Vuuren. This time we've caught you red-handed."

"What? You fucking insurance people are all the same. Tiny suspicious shit-for-brain minds. What ... cough ... what arson?"

"What arson? Do you think I'm blind? Look at that gallon jug of firestarter in your hand, van Vuuren."

"This? It's nothing. I only have it because the fire department wouldn't do their job. The fire chief is paranoid. He trusts no one. He's scared of crocodiles and snakes."

Diefenbaker looked at me and Paul, rolled his eyes, and circled his right temple repeatedly with the tip his index finger.

Paul shook his head at Diefenbaker. "We don't use that language here Mr. Diefenbaker."

Klaas was still speaking. "And who knew that this crappy tabloid newsprint would leak like that? My Naarlen Herald newsprint was better quality for fire starting."

Diefenbaker looked at Paul and said, "I rest my case."

He spiralled a finger around his temple again.

Paul ignored him. Instead, he shouted to Klaas, "Everything's just fine, Klaas. Trust in yourself. And your friends."

"What friends, Paul? Every time I see Pederson, it's a new fucking disaster. He burned down my office, not me. I don't care what I admitted earlier. I lied. You brainwashed me. Pederson's the culprit. He's the reason Trudie isn't with me anymore. I'm going to jump down and stomp on both Pederson and Diefenbaker. By the time I finish, they'll wish they'd never met me. By the time I'm finished, they won't have any parts left to wish with. Do you hear that Diefenbaker and Pederson? *Ik zal op jou graven dansen. Ik zal jou schedels gebruiken als kamerpotten.*"

Paul whispered to me, "That's quite poetic, the last part about using your skulls as pisspots."

Then he turned his attention back to Klaas.

"Don't jump. Breathe, Klaas. Count to three, the way I taught you. Everything will be fine."

"How about my house, Paul? Will that be fucking fine too?"

"Don't sweat the small stuff, Klaas, concentrate on your ... cough ... breathing."

Diefenbaker was climbing down the ladder, still shouting to Klaas.

"I'll see you in court van Vuuren. And your house insurance is now officially null and void, too."

He climbed off the ladder, walked to his car, revved the engine, squealed the tires angrily and left. Perhaps the part about his skull being used as a chamber pot had gotten to him.

"Might be best if you left too, Per," said Paul. "Klaas is overexcited. This kind of setback is very common. Just a bump in the road. To be expected. Normal progression for this type of treatment. Two steps forward one step back. Don't take it personally. He'll be fine again by tomorrow."

"One more for the camera, please, Mr. Pederson, or whoever you are," said the convenience store kid. He took his photo and I left.

At dinner that evening, Inge was staring at the evening edition of the Naarlen Enquirer.

"It says: '*Assassination Attempt at Naarlen Safe House,*' and '*Safe House Burns to Ground; Firefighters Save Mystery Rooftop Man.*'

"Look Per, they have your photo too."

"Really. What does the caption say?"

"It says: '*Is This the Assassin*?' What a stupid rag. How do they make up such nonsense? I only pick it up to read while waiting in line at the supermarket. I don't know why I bother. I much preferred the old Naarlen Herald. And the photo of you is not the best. I wonder if I should send them a better photo. Anyway, tell me about your day, Per, but only good news please. The mood I'm in, I don't want to hear anything negative right now."

"I helped Klaas van Vuuren get his cat off the roof of his house."

"That's nice," said Inge. "You're a good man, Per."

I looked down modestly.

"That's true," I said, then poured us each a glass of wine.

I could end the story there, but remember what I said about women being 60% of my troubles. Let me illustrate how even my hard-earned domestic peace that evening was manipulated by a woman.

After our supper, Inge and I were cuddled companionably on the sitting-room couch. She was doing a crossword puzzle. Every now and then she'd consult her portable phone to look up a word. I was reading when my cell phone buzzed from somewhere in the house.

"Aren't you going to check?" said Inge. "Sounds like a text message on your phone."

"Damn, I was so comfortable, but I should. Where is my cell phone?"

"You left it on the kitchen table, Per."

I heaved myself up and slouched over to the kitchen. I picked up my phone and scrolled to the text messages.

My only new message was from Inge. It said, "While you're up and in the kitchen, bring us back some snacks, would you?"

Women and cats, cats and women. What did I tell you?

*

10. Walking the Dogs

Naarlen is seventy-eight degrees north, square in the Canadian Arctic. You might think it's a remote backwater where nothing happens, but during the July I'm talking about two important naming ceremonies were scheduled there for the same day.

Christine and Eberhardt Kritzinger planned to baptize and officially name their six-month-old daughter. The ceremony was scheduled for an afternoon in the Church of St. Olaf at the top of Harbour Hill Road. It was rumoured that the little girl was to be named Angelica.

St. Olaf has an unusual baptism ceremony—part of the reason for the deep split between the Churches of St. Olaf and St. Birgitta.

Inside St. Birgitta all is rococo; coloured light filters through stained glass windows, the ceiling is painted with elaborate scenes, carvings and gold leaf adorn the walls. At St. Birgitta, the baptisms happen *inside* the church.

The church of St. Olaf is all whitewashed walls and ceilings, clear glass and plain wood. While the first part of the baptism is inside the church, the second part occurs outside—provided the weather allows. Outside, the St. Olafians say, they can glory under

The Creator's own magnificent ceiling, in the glory of His unfiltered light and in His full view. It's a quaint ceremony and any passersby on the street are invited to join in the open-air ceremony. The "Church Outside," the St. Olafians call it, is open to all.

Harbour Hill Road is only gently sloping outside the Church of St. Olaf. Once past the church, the road angles downwards precipitously in a swooping drop to Naarlen Harbour, to Pier One.

The second naming ceremony was scheduled for the same afternoon at the bottom of Harbour Hill Road, in the harbour, at Pier One. The Canadian Coast Guard had built a new medium weight icebreaker to be based in Naarlen. The ship was a miracle of technology with diesel-electric engines, bow thrusters, stern thrusters, helicopter pad, 60 tonne hydraulic crane, 200 tonne winch and davits for launching both a rigid hull inflatable and a Merlin-615 self-righting rescue boat.

The ship had been built and birthed in Halifax, but like the little girl being baptized at the top of the hill, the naming ceremony had been delayed until her arrival in Naarlen Harbour.

By tradition Canadian Coast Guard boats are named either after people, like the CCGS Sir Wilfred Laurier, the CCGS Pierre Radisson, etc., or named after places, like the CCGS Gull Isle, the CCGS Isle Rouge etc.

In a show of political astuteness, the Coast Guard had offered Naarlanders the chance to submit suitable names for the new vessel and to vote on those names. A host of dignitaries stood by for the naming ceremony on Pier One. There was the Commissioner of Nunavut, Madam Elise Kusugak; the Commissioner of the Coast Guard, Commissioner

Benoit; the captain of the unnamed vessel, and Councillor Iqbal Srinivasan, newly returned from stress leave after the incident at last year's Art Fair. Iqbal carried the tally of votes for the various names that Naarlanders had proposed and was to announce the winning name. The Nunavut Commissioner would then do the naming. "I hereby name thee blah blah," according to Iqbal's announcement.

Of the two ceremonies, the infant baptism was dearer to my heart. I know and liked both Eberhardt and Christine and had planned to walk by the St. Olaf Church.

On the morning, though, my friend David Panigoniak phoned.

"Ai, Per."

"Ai, David. What's happening?"

"Could I ask a favour for this afternoon, Per?"

"Ja, ja, David. Sure."

"I was supposed to go round to Claire's aunt. Old Miss Ophelia."

"Ha ha, David! You and Claire?"

"No, no, Per, nothing like that. Just helping a colleague."

"Oh, ja."

"I was going to walk her two dogs for her. She's getting too old and Claire's on duty all day."

"Ja?"

"Only now they've called me in as well."

"Oh. Is there something?"

"You know this afternoon, there's the baptism at the top of Harbour Hill Road and the Coast Guard thing at the bottom of the road?"

"Ja?"

"Well, it's both a crowd problem and a traffic problem."

"We have traffic problems, David? In Naarlen?"

"We do today. Harbour Hill Road is a sheet of ice on the downhill from the church to the harbour."

"So why isn't the road crew out sanding it?"

"Typical Naarlen. The road crew says the icy road is a work hazard. They refuse to go out and sand it until the ice is gone."

"By which stage, no one needs them. *Rasshøler*."

"Tell me about it. Per. Anyhow, we have to block off the top of Harbour Hill Road, just beyond the church where it gets steep. So, I can't walk Aunt Ophelia's dogs. Claire was counting on me. Do you think you could drop by Ophelia and take the dogs? Even if it's a short walk."

"Ja, ja, sure, David. I'll walk them."

I got the address for the old woman from David and turned up there about noon.

"I'm here to walk the dogs, Miss Ophelia."

"What?"

She put a hand to her ear.

I repeated loudly, "I'm here to walk your dogs."

"Oh."

She scanned me and sniffed.

"Why in God's name is my niece going out with you? You're far too old and ugly for her."

"I'm not the one she's going out with."

She sniffed again.

"You must be rich. She's certainly not after you for your looks. Come inside. And don't think I won't talk to her about it. She should have better sense than latching on to you for money alone. Unless she plans to divorce you immediately after and take half. I shall advise her to do that."

"Thank you."

"You'll have some tea before walking the dogs?"

"Nei, nei, thank you. If I drank now, I'd need a washroom while walking the dogs."

"I'll get the cups. At least Claire had the sense to go out with a tea drinker. Do you take milk and sugar?"

"Nei, nei, no tea. Thank you."

"Excellent. Two spoons. And with ouzo. Never trust anyone who takes their tea without. Here."

She handed me a huge mug of tea. We drank.

"I'll introduce you to the dogs then, young man."

She whistled. Two beasts the size of Percheron stallions appeared. They gazed down at me. One of them drooled as though I was dinner. The other wrinkled its nose as though I wasn't good enough for dinner.

"This is Boreas, and this is Notus. My two dogs."

"Nice doggies," I said to them weakly.

They wrinkled their foreheads in surprise. The dinner speaks?

"They look more like horses, Miss Ophelia."

"Very astute, young man. So few youngsters know their Greek mythology. I shall let my niece know that you have at least that redeeming quality, in spite of your ouzo-guzzling habit and decrepit features."

"Thank you."

"Boreas and Notus were the North and South Wind, of course, in mythology. They took the shape horses. They pulled Zeus's chariot."

"Zeus?"

"Precisely young, man. I'm so glad you didn't give him his Roman name. Another meagre point in your dishevelled favour."

"Thank you."

I bowed.

"The Romans were trumped-up Johnny-come-latelies. Nouveau riche. My family is Greek and proud of it. The old aristocracy. From Piraeus. What do you say to that, dissipated young man?"

"Piraeus, ja, ja. Very good."

"Yes, it is. Can't stand Romans. Are you Roman?"

"Nei, nei, not Roman, Ma'am."

"Not Egyptian, are you? Can't stand them either. They claim they taught the Greeks everything. All nonsense. They knew nothing except triangles and playing with sand. Couldn't even figure out rectangles, squares and rhombuses. All they did was pyramids. Triangles against triangles."

"Nei, nei, Ma'am. Neither Egyptian nor Roman."

"Macedonian? Persian? Sumerian? Assyrian? Can't stand them either."

"Nei, nei, Ma'am. And the Sumerians are all dead."

"Good thing too. And you're not one of the others?"

"Nei."

"Hmm, well, I'm sure there are plenty of other reasons why I dislike you."

"Thank you."

"Anyway. Here are their leashes. Go have your walk. I'll be glad to get them out of the house for a while. And you. Especially you."

"Thank you."

"Oh, and take these poop and scoop bags."

She gave me two bags, each as big as those body bags you see in the morgue scenes in crime movies.

I left. The first part of the walk was fine. The dogs were on those long retractable leashes—the kind that you can extend or roll back up like a surveyor's measuring tape. With the dogs behaving so well, I hooked the retractable leashes to my belt. I aimed us for the Eberhardt and Christine baptism.

I wouldn't be able to go inside with the two dogs, but at least I could participate in the outdoor ceremony. I was just in time.

Father René Guillaume was leading the congregation out from the church into the street. Christine and Eberhardt were right behind him holding the infant girl. All three were walking gingerly. Even here on the almost flat part of Harbour Hill Road there were large areas of slippery ice.

René paused in the middle of the road. The congregation circled him. The dogs paused in puzzlement. One moved to the right-hand edge of the street to look past the congregation. The other moved to the left edge. I saw a policewoman placing orange warning cones across the road a few metres beyond the congregation, just before the road dropped into its steep descent. She looked familiar. Of course! Policewoman Claire.

The dogs spotted her and moved toward her, slowly at first, noses up, sniffing for final confirmation that it was their old friend, their owner's niece. I tugged at their leashes. It was about as effective as a fly trying to stop a horse. I dug my heels into the ground. Black ice. I slid forward toward the congregation, one leash girdling their left side, one leash girdling their right side.

The dogs broke into a run of joyous recognition. Their leashes were fully extended and so taut that there was no hope of unclipping them from my belt.

I collided with the rear edge of the congregation. To my left and right, others were being dragged forward by the encircling leashes.

Father René at the centre, and still ignorant of the calamity behind, held the girl up high above the crowd.

"How is this infant to be named?"

"AYEEE ...," screamed the rear half of the crowd as we all compressed and gathered speed.

"How pretty," said René. "Does it have a meaning?"

"GOOD GOD! SAVE THE CHILD."

"How beautiful," said René. Then he too was caught up in the great sliding mass of people.

It all happened too quickly. Ice does that. The dogs reached Claire at the brink of the downhill.

Like all overenthusiastic mutts, they overshot, and found themselves on a sheet of steep ice. Scrabble as the might, they had no purchase. Their weight pulled them down the hill regardless of their frantic paddling. I and the whole congregation, tightly wrapped in the two dog leashes like fish caught in a trawl net, went with them.

There was a slow-mo moment as the congregation teetered on the crest of the road just before the steep part. Here, the road was not yet entirely iced over. Here friction on a few non-icy spots, and the mass of the congregation in the trawl net was a partial counterbalance to the pull of the dogs below us.

We held our breaths. It must be what swimmers and boaters feel when they've ventured too close to the top edge of Niagara Falls. For a brief moment all hangs in the balance. For a brief moment, the swimmers think they can thrash and kick their way back to safety. For a brief moment hope—almost relief—flourishes.

"Ah," say the swimmers in shaky, false triumph, "that was close, but I had it under control all the time."

And then, despite their treacherous relief and useless thrashing, the implacable current grips, so seemingly slow at first, yet so ineluctable, then speeds them and tosses them over the edge.

We too edged irrevocably forward, caught in our unrelenting trawl net. The front edge of the congregation disappeared over the downward crest of the road. Our resistance to the forward current weakened and our speed increased each time another member slid forward and down.

"AYEE... AYEE... SAVE THE CHILD... GIVE ME MY BABY... WHAT'S HAPPENING... MY GLASSES... GOD SAKE... QUIT PUSHING AT THE BACK... I CAN'T HELP IT... DON'T BLASPHEME... DON'T... GOD'S SAKE... DON'T FUCKING BLASPHEME... DON'T PANIC... IT'S FINE... NO, IT ISN'T... GET MY GLASSES... STOP PUSHING... AYEE... AYEE."

In that slo-mo moment at the crest of the road, I considered whether, even though I couldn't unclip the leashes, I could at least undo my belt. The tension on the thing was enormous, but I got it open. It didn't help. With one leash firmly hooked to the left side of my belt and one leash firmly hooked to the right side, the belt wasn't coming off my trousers. All that happened was that my trousers dropped to mid-thigh.

I clutched at them grimly. It was bad enough that I was going be killed in the madcap descent into the sea; at least I wanted some dignity in my death. Inge would kill me if I were found dead with trousers around my ankles. Trousers at mid-thigh are more dignified on a drowned and frozen corpse than trousers around the ankles.

Also, with trousers around the ankles, onlookers—at least in Naarlen—will make up stupid phrases like, "He couldn't leave it alone, even in death."

Policewoman Claire was standing at the side of the road staring in frozen horror as we shot past her. I covered my face with one arm, hoping she wouldn't recognize me. I would have put both arms up, but I needed the other arm for my trousers.

David hadn't exaggerated when he said the road down was pure ice. I understood now why the road crew wouldn't touch it. I don't think I've ever slid so fast. I've been on giant rollercoasters down south, but this road made them look tame. At every hump in the road the entire congregation went airborne, then thumped back down hard, all still caught in the same trawl net. At least with rollercoasters you know everyone will survive the ride. At the speed we were going down the road, I had doubts. The two dogs added their soundtrack by howling all the way down like air raid sirens.

We accelerated all the gut-twisting way down that horrible luge run, and we were still accelerating, like bullets exiting a rifle barrel, when we hit the bottom. We should have shot off the bottom of the road, across Pier One, and into the icy sea. With the water at freezing point or below, it would have been a mass drowning. No rescue effort would have reached all of us in time.

What saved us was the crowd on the pier, gathered for the naming of the Coast Guard icebreaker. We plowed into them the way a well-aimed bowling ball scatters the pins in a bowling alley. People, fists and curses flew every which way.

Up at the front of the crowd, on a little stage by the water's edge stood the dignitaries. Councillor Iqbal was announcing through a booming loudspeaker, "And the winning name for the ship is..."

The wind was from the sea, and may have muted our howling descent. It couldn't mute the scene of chaos as we plowed into the crowd.

There was a moment's stunned silence after the mass impact. I was the first to stand up, not because I was less bruised than the others, but merely because I had greater guilt and a greater need to run.

It wasn't a good strategy. I found I was standing alone, trousers lowered, in a sea of scattered, downed skittles as Iqbal paused after "And the winning name for the ship is..."

He stared at me in horror and pointed. "It's that fucking Per!"

The Nunavut commissioner and the Coast Guard commissioner stared at each other. You don't rise to be commissioners without knowing how to weasel out of a messy situation.

They nodded at each other. Madam Elise Kusugak lost no time. She stepped to the microphone and announced, "I hereby name this vessel the 'Fecund Pear.' God bless all who sail in her."

The ship's captain popped the champagne cork and filled four glasses. The tradition of smashing the bottle against the ship's bow is still alive and well elsewhere, but not when the Coast Guard could nab you for littering broken glass on the sea floor.

The front rank of the crowd, the only part unscathed, clapped enthusiastically.

Madame Elise; Pierre Benoit, the Coast Guard Commissioner, and the captain of the "Fecund Pear" raised their glasses and drank.

A camera flash illuminated the moment. It was the kid from the convenience store, the one who had previously photographed me for the Naarlen Enquirer. He caught the two commissioners toasting the new ship.

Iqbal was still frozen in place, his arm pointing at where I'd risen from the crowd.

As soon as the photo moment had passed, Benoit offered his arm to Madam Kusugak. "We should be going; our car is waiting."

He turned to Iqbal and the ship's captain.

"I'd love to stay but Madam Elise and I have pressing business elsewhere. I'll let you two take care of whatever is happening at the back of the crowd. Right? Very good. Carry on."

They left. I've rarely seen a political retreat and delegation of a hot potato executed so smoothly.

I got the leashes off my belt, raised my trousers, tied the dogs to a fence and ran to the nearby public washroom. The terror of the descent plus all the tea and ouzo I'd been forced to drink needed an outlet. My knees were too rubbery for standing at the urinal so I sat trembling in a stall for the next half hour.

When I emerged most of the crowd had gone. Two council road workers were lounging nearby.

"So, what happened here?" I asked them, feigning ignorance.

"Big church congregation slid down the ice," said the first one, a fellow named Arthur whom I knew slightly.

"What caused it, Arthur?"

"Ice caused it. We warned everybody. Asked the police to block off the road and warn people. Bloody police sat on their arses and did dick-all. As usual."

"Ah ha, ja, ja, dick-all. Anyone hurt?"

"Couple of scrapes, bruises, some hysterics. No breaks, nothing serious. Fair amount of boasting."

"Boasting, Arthur? Nei, nei, what boasting?"

He spat.

"You know how it is. The women admit being terrified, the men feel they have to say how it was all great fun and they'd willingly do it again."

"Again? Are they crazy?"

"Oh, yes, big talk about how much fun it was, and if only the course was properly sandbagged at the bottom and padded on the sides it should be an annual Naarlen event. With a cup for the fastest time. They'd happily compete."

"Really?"

"S'all big talk, Per. You know? They'd happily compete, just not right now thank you, because they have to go home and change underwear first."

"Hah ha, underwear, ja. And the little baby girl? Is she alright, Arthur?"

"Name of Ayee. Right pretty name. Wish I'd thought of that for our little one. Right as rain she is. Not a hair out of place."

"*Gudskjelov*. Thank God. Well, must be off. Nice chatting to you, Arthur."

I untied the dogs and started walking away when the other road worker shouted, "Hey, you!"

My heart sank. Had I been rumbled after all? Is this where the mob from St. Olaf appears with pitchforks to lynch me?

"Ja, what?"

"Pick up your dog poop."

"Oh."

I stooped and scooped and disposed of the giant load into a nearby trash container. Then I walked the dogs back to Miss Ophelia. Obviously not via Harbour Hill Road.

"There you are," said Miss Ophelia. "You look even uglier than when I first saw you. Didn't think that was possible. My niece must be blind. Runs in her family. Her father wore glasses. Couldn't tell grass from cow turds without them. Always made him leave his shoes outside. You can come inside if your shoes are turd-free. If you must."

I handed her the dog leashes without crossing the threshold.

"Nei, nei, nei," I said.

I don't drink, and ouzo in tea is even more disgusting than ouzo without tea. Also, I was shaking with anger at her, her dogs, and her insults, so I lied.

"My family is from Sparta, Miss Ophelia. We whomped the Athenians and Piraeus in the year 405 BC. Maybe your family forgot? And your dogs are a public menace."

It should have been satisfying, but she merely put her hand to her ear and said, "Don't mumble. You're from Djakarta and you have a dog called Denis? I don't give a damn for Djakarta, and what kind of moron calls his dog, 'Denis'? I shall speak to my niece about this."

I left.

I caught up with David the next day and confessed everything. He shook with laughter.

"You don't know half the story, Per."

"What half?"

"Claire introduced me to Ophelia last night as her boyfriend..."

"Oh, David, congratulations. She's lovely. I'm mean Claire. Not Ophelia."

"Yes, but you have to keep it quiet. It wouldn't look good at work. I know I can rely on you, Per."

"Ja, ja, sure."

"But that's not the story, Per. Claire was nervous about introducing me to Ophelia. Ophelia thinks no one is good enough for Claire unless they're Greek."

"Ja?"

"Well, for some reason Ophelia dislikes you. I mean, she dislikes you even beyond the fact that you're not Greek."

"Oh. That's bad."

"No, Per. It's not bad, it's wonderful. She's an old woman. Cantankerous. Who knows what she likes or dislikes? But she was so relieved to hear that I was the boyfriend, not you, that she loves me. It's an Einstein thing. Relativity. Compared to you, she loves me. Didn't even ask if I was Greek. I can't thank you enough."

"Ja, nei, that's not entirely heart-warming, David. I mean I'm glad she likes you, but..."

"Don't worry Per, my friend. She's a confused woman. She thought you were an Indonesian and that you have a dog named Denis. Claire had a hard time keeping a straight face."

"Does Claire know that it was me with the dogs at the top of Harbour Hill Road?"

"Yes, of course. She says she's very sorry the dogs misbehaved and ran to her. She feels she's to blame."

"Ja, ja. Well. Let's say no more about it. I won't tell anyone if she doesn't."

"No. We don't have to say anything. I talked to the congregation. No one has a clear idea of what happened. It was all too fast and too scary. Some people know you were there but they think you were pushed too."

"*Herregud.* It *was* scary. I have to tell Inge something, not everything, not about my trousers, she won't like that, and Bernie..."

"Of course, Per, Bernie will already have figured it all out."

I caught up with Bernie, our mayor and publican, at "The Other Tooth" two days later over a cup of coffee.

"Per, the town should thank you again."

"Ja? Why's that Bernie?"

"You're the founding father of our annual Harbour Hill Road Ice Race. I take it you'll enter next year? City council has already approved big prizes and some safety barriers."

"Nei, nei, Bernie. I'm not going near it. Did Councillor Iqbal agree to this? He seemed a bit angry when it happened."

"Councillor Iqbal has gone back on stress leave. He came back to work too early. Not fully cured yet. Don't worry about him. You should be proud. Who else has ever named both a beautiful baby girl and a brand-new ship all on the same day? Incidentally, the baby girl smiled all the way down the ice. She'll be fearless when she grows up."

There you have the story. Even among Naarlanders, few know the complete version. After all these years, I need to finally set it down because it's a piece of Canadian history. Canadiana as they say. The answer to a Canadian maritime mystery.

People keep asking, "How amongst all the names like 'Martha L. Black,' 'Samuel Risley,' 'Sir John Franklin,' 'Des Groseillers,' 'Hudson' and the like did the Coast Guard acquire a ship named 'The Fecund Pear'?"

Somewhere someone should record the answer. History should know. I'm recording the answer here, for posterity, for future historians, for future generations. This is how it happened, and now you know too.

*

11. The Sound of the Pin

When you live as far north as Inge and I and all the other Naarlanders do, that is to say seventy-eight degrees north, travel arrangement can be capricious. I know, capricious also a good word for Naarlenders, but right now I'm talking about travel plans.

I recall an August when Inge, my wife flew down south to celebrate her mother's seventieth birthday. That's seventy measured in human years because I don't know the correct number in crocodile years.

I respect my mother-in-law, in the same way that I respect the chainsaw that I occasionally borrow from Grampa McVee, or the way I respect any other lethal power tool that I'm entirely untrained to work with.

McVee's chainsaw is a wonderful piece of engineering but you need to wear protective gear, and once you get it warmed up, don't expect to get a word in edgewise. Worse, if you as much as sneeze wrong, it will take your head off. So, when Inge asked if I wanted to come down south with her for her mother's birthday, I declined.

"Someone has to look after Attila," I said.

Inge gave me a needlessly long look. Attila incidentally, is the name of Inge's cat, not her mother, though it fits both.

The weather changed every hour, as did Inge's flight plans out of Naarlen. Three days in a row she went to our little airport under blue skies only to be sent home under howling winds, whiteouts of blowing snow and ice, and temperatures so low that de-icing the plane wasn't remotely possible. On the fourth day, the airport called our home phone at four a.m.

"We've got a brief window for takeoff. If you can get here in the next half hour, we'll get you on the flight.

We were both groggy with sleep.

"It's 4 a.m., Inge."

"Is it? Don't be angry, Per. I suppose it's a blessing, if I can finally go. I barely know what day it is any more."

She got to the airport and texted me from the runway.

"Finally going. You'll be at August Fest the same day as I'm at Mom's birthday. Miss you. Love, Inge."

When you live as far north as Naarlen, the long dark winters wear on you. That's why in early August Naarlanders have a celebration. August Fest. It's an excuse, a means to get our spirits up in advance of the coming winter brutality.

Naarlen is not big. There are two venues in which to have a moderately large indoor celebration. One is the Naarlen high school gymnasium, the other is the entry hall of the Naarlen Museum.

If you're wondering why I didn't say Museum of Science or Museum of Natural History or Museum of Textiles and Wooden Clog Manufacturing or Museum of whatever, it's because the Naarlen Museum is most of those things in one. Not clog manufacturing, obviously.

There's a section on mining technology featuring Naarlen's platinum and palladium ores and descriptions of the mining techniques used in Naarlen's mines. It includes a dummy figure of a rescue miner—a draegerman with helmet, mask, helmet light, boots, first-aid kit, overalls and emergency breathing apparatus.

There's a section describing Naarlen's key role as an aviation weather forecasting station during WWII plus a display of the island's military defences of the time. This includes a weather sonde balloon, a Canadian soldier's uniform, an air-cooled, heavy barrel Browning machine gun mounted on a simple snow sled, a mills grenade, and a mess kit.

There's a section on kayak building showing how Inuit kayaks are framed and covered in skin, and how more modern kayaks are built.

There's a section on Arctic ptarmigans and how, in bad storms, they hunker down deliberately to let the drifting snow cover and insulate them.

Inge's mother, who comes from money, had booked the very fancy Chicago Museum of Modern Art for her birthday bash on the same day as Naarlen's August Fest. The Naarlen Museum is low tech. Climate and humidity control are basic. We're not protecting the Mona Lisa here. There is no modern style interaction for visitors. There are no high-tech buttons, computer simulations, screens or other interactive tools. The exhibits sit on one side of a rope. Viewers stand on the other side of the rope and gaze at the exhibits and descriptive texts.

If you want museums with computer simulations and immersive three-D holograms, stay down south or go to my mother-in-law's birthday bash. Me? I love our Naarlen Museum and the good folks who run it. They're creative and put on a great show with minimal resources. Geniuses, all of them.

There was a fair crowd for our August Fest—couple of hundred people, circulating with drinks and snacks. The weather was unseasonably warm. With so many people, the hall grew too hot. Aarne and I jammed open the entrance doors of the museum to let some cooler air in, then retreated deeper into the hall. Aarne is Naarlen's tailor and dry cleaner. His mutt, Magnus, was sitting outside. Magnus is dumb, but at least understands "Wait outside" if it's repeated every fifteen minutes.

If you've followed any of my stories so far, you'll know that my experience with dogs has not been the best.

My previous experience with Magnus in particular was holding him for the vet. He bit me. I mean, it was Magnus who bit me, not the vet who bit me, and I ended up swallowing Magnus's medication. I'm not overly fond of Magnus. Aarne is OK. He's still deeply grateful to me for taking Magnus to the vet. Considering everything that happened to me on that occasion, I understand why he's grateful.

Aarne is, amongst other things, a chess fanatic. He was droning on about some chess anecdote when a woman in a bright red dress briefly stepped between us, pressed something into my hand then disappeared into the crowd.

"And so, Per, the grandmaster said, 'Actually, I do.' Ha ha. How about that?"

Aarne could have been babbling about how to unclog toilets on Mars for all I cared at that moment. I was looking at the object that had just been pushed into my hand.

It was the Mills grenade from the museum's display.

Satan! Fy Faen!

Normally the thing is on a display board with a protective layer of clear acrylic glass screwed down over it. But how hard is it to unscrew three screws? All you need is a screwdriver and two minutes unsupervised. Why don't these museum shitheads in Naarlen have better security? I recall reading somewhere how the explosive used in these things becomes so unstable with the years that just shouting too loudly can set them off.

The shouting danger was top of mind, because Aarne gets louder and louder when you don't pay attention to his endless chess stories.

"Per, LISTEN. The grandmaster said, 'ACTUALLY I DO.' Ha ha. Ha ha ha. GET IT?"

"*Hold kjef, Aarne!*"

Aarne is Swedish, but the Swedish and Norwegian for "shut it" is similar. He looked hurt. Better hurt than dead.

I charged for the door and threw the grenade as far out into the snow as I could.

I turned back shaking with rage and delayed fear. Who was the woman in red who'd done this? And why? I hadn't paid attention to her face. Grenades have a way of diverting the eye. The brief impression was of someone I didn't know or didn't know well. Unattractive or maybe just poorly groomed. I scanned the room for red dress.

There! Red dress. Back to me. Alone. Trying to hide in the crowd.

I charged, clamped both my arms around her waist and said triumphantly, "Got you! Not letting go either."

She turned to face me.

This was a face I knew very well, not some stranger. Beautiful, immaculately groomed. Olga Harkonnen, and definitely not the woman who'd pushed the grenade into my hands, although Olga too had previously threatened me with violence.

I had caught the wrong red dress woman.

Olga and I stared at each other. We both froze. Then Olga smiled slowly, closed her eyes briefly in resignation and leaned her forehead against my chest.

"Per."

"Olga."

"Per, I tried to keep you at a distance ... because I didn't want to... Inge's my friend... I didn't want to be tempted... I thought you believed my threats... I thought you'd be scared off..."

We had rotated a half turn. My view was now back, through the crowd, out the museum doors. Aarne's dog was sniffing in the snow. He picked something up in his jaws, something dark and round, he was headed back to the museum doors. Would he remember, "stay outside"?

"Per... I can't fight this ... say something to me ... please."

Her arms were around my waist, her hands on my back, stroking my back.

"Um..."

I squinted. What the hell was Magnus carrying in his mouth? I had a sinking feeling. It was hard to concentrate on what Olga was saying.

"You're here alone, Per?"

"Yes. Alone."

"Where's Inge?"

"She's gone. Didn't you know?"

"Gone?"

"Gone. A long, lingering, drawn-out departure. When it finally happened, she no longer even knew what day of the week it was. 'It's a blessing, don't be angry, Per,' she said to me. And then, suddenly, she was gone. She is with her mother now. In a better place than this."

"Oh, Per. I had no idea. I'm so sorry."

The dog was getting closer to the museum. What WAS he carrying?

"So, you're alone now, Per?"

Damn it, Magnus, the dog was coming through the museum doors. I no longer had any doubt what he was carrying in his jaws. My entire attention was on him. Something told me he'd be looking for me. My replies to Olga were on autopilot from some remote planet. I have no idea what sense they made.

"So, you're alone now, Per?" she repeated.

"I'm about to take the loneliest walk that any human can take," I said.

Whether by grenade or other means, you always exit this world alone.

"Oh, Per."

"Until death."

I calculated that would be about thirty seconds at most, but Olga's back was to the dog. She didn't see him. English isn't my natural language, and even if it were, it's hard to explain this kind of thing as you see the jaws of death approaching. Magnus looked around for the person who'd thrown this new toy for him. He spotted me. He started walking towards me. The grenade was big, but he's a big dog. It was no problem for him. He was drooling with the joy of the game. Or drooling with the joy of having upped the game from merely biting Per to killing Per with a grenade.

"Per," said Olga, "You don't have to walk alone. I know before, that other time, I was going to meet you in secret behind Inge's back. But that's no longer good enough for me. Even if Inge were still here with us, secret meetings would no longer be enough. If we're going to do this, I want it to be out in the open, no secrets, no hiding it from anyone. You feel the same, don't you? I'm not deceiving myself about our feelings for each other?"

"Ja, ja, for sure..."

Who knows what that answer meant. My mouth was on autopilot. Maybe it meant that getting the grenade out into the open, out of the museum was what I wanted.

Normally, in Olga's presence, my eyes and ears would see and hear nothing and no one but her. And holding her, being held by her, gazing into her eyes would be a dream. But tonight, my eyes and ears were tuned to nothing and no one but the damned dog. My ears may have heard Olga, but my brain was incapable of processing whatever it was that she was wittering on about. Magnus, the dog, was homing in on me like a heat-seeking missile. Behind him I saw *the* woman in red, the assassin who'd pressed the grenade into my hand, scampering out of the museum door. I finally recognized her. Sheilagh Smith. The one who'd put a lock with my name on the harbour bridge, the one who'd previously pushed me and Olga into the harbour for ignoring all the cards she'd sent me.

"I knew it," said Olga happily, tightening her arms around me. "You feel it too. Per. No more sordid secrecy. That's why you chose this occasion to approach me, to put your arms around me. You want to announce your feelings ... your love ... our love ... to the whole room, don't you? I would have been happy with a more private discussion, but if that's what you want, let's do it. This moment was meant to be."

She raised her voice. "Quiet everyone, please. Per has something he wants to tell you."

Olga has a beautiful, distinctive voice and a commanding presence. The room and all two hundred people grew quiet almost immediately. At the same moment, Magnus dropped the grenade at my feet, more precisely he dropped it behind Olga's feet. She didn't see that. I did. The rest of the room did. Magnus looked up at me waiting for me to repeat the game of throw and fetch.

The room was so quiet you could have heard a pin drop. Which was exactly what I heard. A pin dropping. From the grenade to the floor.

"Tell them, Per," whispered Olga, gazing at me tenderly, "tell them about our feelings for each other."

"EVERYBODY GET OUT!!" I shouted at the room. "GET OUT! GET OUT! GET OUT NOW!"

Olga's head jerked in shock.

"You ... you ... you BASTARD!"

There were tears starting down her beautiful cheeks. I wondered how, with death lying at our feet,

I still had time to notice the beauty of her cheeks, eyes and voice.

"You heartless MONSTER, playing games with my feelings! Why? Why Per? Why are you doing this?"

"Come quickly," I said, sidestepping the grenade and trying to pull her towards the exit.

"With YOU? NEVER!"

She was beating at my face with her fists.

"Olga, come, PLEASE, now."

She changed to banging my chest with fists.

"NEVER. MONSTER, MONSTER, MONSTER!"

I searched hurriedly for some phrase to calm her and dry the tears on those lovely cheeks.

"You stupid cow, you'll kill us both!"

Admittedly, with more preparation it might have been better. I was trying to move her towards the exit. She pulled back.

"MONSTER! Why did I ever think ..."

In desperation I somehow managed to sling her over my shoulder and half ran half shuffled towards the door. It was like those nightmares where you're running from something and your legs are barely moving. Not only was Olga's weight slowing me, but I was running eyes mostly closed to avoid her fist beating at my face. Her other fist was pulling at my hair. You wouldn't think hair-pulling would interfere with running, it's rarely mentioned in runners' magazines or training log books. But it does slow you down. Take it from an expert. There's a reason no Olympic sprinter has ever won a medal while someone pulls at their hair. Also, she was trying to knee me in the chest. And anyway, my own knees were rubber with panic.

I realized that her head, positioned behind my shoulder, would take the full brunt of the grenade. I swung around and ran backwards. It would slow us down, but at least her head would be shielded.

I could feel Olga shaking with huge, body-shaking sobs; sobbing so hard she could barely get enough breath. It was heartbreaking.

Meanwhile, Magnus was trotting next to me, still looking up expectantly with a big doggy smile on his stupid, fucking face:

"I fetched it. Did you see? Did you see, Mister? Who's a good dog? Me. I'm a good dog. Where's the treat? Treat now, please, Mister. Gratification delayed is gratification denied. Treat, please. After the treat can we do it again? Throw the grenade again, Mister. After the treat. For the good dog."

I hate dogs. All that enthusiasm and tail-wagging when I'm going to die. Thank God he'd left the grenade lying where he'd dropped it.

"Per you ... sob ... agonized inhalation ... sob... MONSTER. PUT ME DOWN N..."

Then the explosion lifted us off my feet and things went hazy.

My first semi-coherent memory after that was in a hospital bed. I tried to move my limbs and feel my more private appendages. There seemed to be the right number of each. Just sore. I looked sideways. Olga was in the bed next to mine, either asleep or unconscious. Then I slept. Probably drugs.

When I woke, Sergeant Panigoniak was seated by my bedside.

"Ai, David. Qanuipit?"

"Ai, Per. Better question is, how are you?"

"Fuzzy. There's a ringing in my ears and my throat is sore. Sheilagh Smith did it."

"We know. We have it all on the museum security video. There's an arrest warrant out for Sheilagh.

We're looking for her. You and Olga were lucky the grenade was so old. It exploded with reduced force. You and Olga both have cuts and some stitches in your legs. Magnus was unhurt."

"Fucking Magnus. I hate him. I hate all dogs. And those fucking museum assholes, David. I hate them too. Shouldn't be allowed to run a toy store, never mind a real museum, keeping a live grenade on display."

"True. Lucky thing Sheilagh didn't use the machine gun."

"Don't tell me. The museum idiots had live ammunition for that?"

"Enough for another massacre."

I looked to my right. The bed was empty.

"David, where's Olga?"

"Only stitches on her leg, like I said. You did a good job getting her out. She's just angry. Like a beehive someone's been beating on."

"Oh. Did they release her?"

"Not yet. They will."

I pointed to the empty bed.

"Why isn't she there?"

"She woke up before you. Ripped the IV tube out of your arm and tried to strangle you with it. A nurse intervened. They have her in a different ward right now."

"She's angry at ME? Not at Sheilagh?"

"Yes. I explained to her about Sheilagh and the grenade, Per, but she doesn't care about the grenade or nearly being killed. Called it trivial, a red herring, a non-event. She's angry at something you said, or did."

"Oh. Something I did that's worse than being killed by a grenade?"

"So she says, Per."

"David, I didn't do anything. I swear."

"Then it's something you didn't do, or didn't say. You want to press charges, Per? For the attempted strangulation with the IV line?"

I had a lump in my throat at the thought of Olga being angry with me yet again. What had I done wrong this time? I was close to tears.

"Charges, David? Against, Olga? No, I couldn't. Never. Olga's wonderful ... really ... a wonderful woman... I mean person ... well woman too, obviously... I know that she's ... a woman as well as a person ... a once in a lifetime treasure. Strangling me was just overreacting ... to some little... I don't know... We'll sort it out ... she and I."

"OK, Per, I'll let her know, no charges. Maybe you should give it some time before you try to sort anything out with her? A cooling off period? Keep your distance for a while?"

Herregud. Again.

If my arms hadn't been connected to various tubes, I would have done a double face-palm.

"Where's Inge, David?"

"I don't know, Per. Somewhere down south, isn't she? She knows nothing of this. I have no contact info for her. You want to give me her number? Want me to call her?"

"No, thanks, David."

The next visitor was the kid from the convenience store. The one who takes photos for the Naarlen Enquirer.

"Hello Mr. Pederson, or whoever you are, can I take your photo?"

"Whatever. I never heard your name."

"Sampath Ranasinghe. You can call me 'Sam,' Mr. Pederson."

He took my photo.

"About the grenade and the attempted assassination, are you organized crime, Mr. Pederson?"

"Nei. You should see the state of my desk. I can never find anything."

"Are you in a witness protection program?"

"Nei, nei, not witness protection. I'm in hospital from a grenade blast. Do I look protected?"

"Have you ever been to Tennessee, Mr. Pederson?"

"Nei. Racist, xenophobic, dogmatic, fundamentalist Deep South USA. Who would want to go there?"

"You're not Elvis then. What can you tell me about the Mothers of Invention?"

"It was a virgin birth, Sam."

"What?"

"Think, Sam. Necessity was the mother. Who was the father of invention?"

"The father? There wasn't one, Mr. Pederson."

"Exactly, Sam. Parthenogenesis. The biological term for a virgin birth."

"Are you on drugs Mr. Pederson?"

I glanced at the IV tube and drip bag. There was some twelve-syllable incomprehensible label taped on the drip bag. More than just saline solution.

"Ja, ja, drugs. Sure. Lots of them. With names I can't pronounce."

"I meant Frank Zappa's rock band, the 'Mothers of Invention.' Clearly, you're not Salman Rushdie. He was a fan of the Mothers."

"Was he, Sam?"

"Oh, yes. Rushdie was at the Royal Albert Hall for one of their big concerts. He writes about it. I'm a

Rushdie fan, so now I too listen to Frank Zappa and The Mothers of Invention."

We stared at each other uncomprehendingly.

"So, Mr. Pederson, readers at the Naarlen Enquirer want to know why someone wanted to assassinate you."

"God knows. Ask him."

"Thank you, Mr. Pederson. You've been very helpful."

Three hours later I was allowed to go home. I didn't want to show my face in public so I mooched around indoors. For lack of anything better to do, I fed Attila, changed the water in his bowl, trimmed his claws, cleaned his litter box, combed him and bought a carton of milk for him.

An hour later, a taxi pulled up. Inge got out. She gave me a big kiss. She had her bags in one hand and the Naarlen Enquirer in the other.

I squinted at the front page of the Enquirer while we hugged. It carried a large photo of Olga, me and Magnus, taken just as Magnus was dropping the grenade behind Olga. The heading and lead read:

"Virgin-Birth Cult Attempts Mass Suicide
Pederson says attempt was on God's orders."

The caption under the photo said:

"Cult leader, Per Pederson, self-confessed drug user and well known to Naarlen Police."

"Hi, Per."

"Hi, Sweetie."

She noticed me squinting at the Enquirer.

"Such trash, I don't know why I bother. What is this 'Virgin-Birth Cult'? Do they mean Christianity? It's beyond a cult by now, and I should tell them you're not the leader unless you became pope while I was away. I really should get them a better picture of you."

"Hah, ja, ja, such nonsense. Better picture, sure. You're home early."

"Oh, Per. I had such a row with my mother."

"Really?"

"Yes, she said I shouldn't have left you alone here because you'd find a way to make a mess of something. Of everything. I said you only had to look after Attila while I was gone. You did, didn't you, Per? Look after Attila? Please, God, say you did. I couldn't bear it if my mother was right. She's so smug."

"Ja, ja, see for yourself, Inge. Go look at his water bowl, his litter and..."

She ran to the basement to look. I heard exclamations of pleasure. She ran back up from the basement beaming.

"Oh, Per, I'm so grateful to you. You have no idea."

"Did you see that..."

"Yes, I saw his claws and..."

"And his coat..."

"And water bowl and the litter box. I'm going to send photos to my mother. I'm so happy. I don't know why she says you can't be left alone."

"Pish. Your mother, she's a dear woman, but overly suspicious of me."

"I know Per. I'm sorry. You're such a good man. She was so sure of herself, can you believe, she even had me half persuaded that you'd be creating some disaster."

"Disaster?" My anger at Inge's mother was morphing into a swelling rage at Inge and her betrayal of me.

"Your mother persuaded you? You believed her? Inge, how could you? And what disasters? When have I ever ...?"

"Who knows, what she was thinking, or making me think. Ridiculous, I know. Will you forgive me, Per?"

When she holds my hand and gazes at me like that, she can ask anything.

"Come Per, sit yourself down here. I'll make us a nice cup of coffee and we can sit together and cuddle."

I heard her rummaging in the kitchen. The fridge door opened.

"Oh, Per, you're such a sweetheart. You even bought a new carton of milk for my return. You're the best. What would I or Naarlen do without you?"

She's right, of course. What would they do without me? But one must be modest. I made no reply, merely smiled.

***

A Word to the Reader

Dear Reader,

If you've come this far with me, thank you. I hope you enjoyed our voyage together.

I'm an indie author: I've chosen to do all the work on this book myself, from the first blank page until the final chapter in your hands. There is no literary agency or large publishing house involved. It's old-style artisan work, like the village blacksmith or potter.

And like the village blacksmith, there is no marketing agency. The essential marketing for any indie author is your testimony.

If you enjoyed the book, please take two minutes to leave a review on Amazon or Goodreads or on your favourite book review site. The process on most of these sites is simple (you can even use a pen name if you like). Thousands do it. It makes a big difference.

Thank you.
Peter Staadecker,
Toronto, Canada.

Acknowledgements

My thanks to my family, especially my wife, for giving me the space and time to write. Also, thanks to my friend, Daphne Cooper. Daphne and I have for several years had a short story writing challenge ping-ponging back and forth between us. Naarlen began as a short story in response to such a challenge and grew into something larger, thanks to Daphne's encouragement.

Author Information

At time of writing this, books by Peter Staadecker include:

The Twelve Man Bilbo Choir (A novel of justice, injustice, tragedy and love inspired by actual events that changed legal history)

The Illyrian Voyages, Book I: **Dropping into Darkness** (An Eco-Sci-Fi fantasy)

The Illyrian Voyages, Book 2: **A Glimmer of Light** (An Eco-Sci-Fi fantasy)

Just One More Page (For children aged six to ten years old)

For updates, please visit http://publishing.staadecker.com

Fan? Or want to be on the distribution list about Peter's next books? Drop Peter a note. (Please do not send plot suggestions, though. Plot suggestions will be deleted unread.) You can reach Peter via:

- https://publishing.staadecker.com/#contact
- https://www.facebook.com/staadecker.books
- https://twitter.com/PeterStaadecker

www.ingramcontent.com/pod-product-compliance
Lightning Source LLC
LaVergne TN
LVHW020711110826
845149LV00012B/2206

* 9 7 8 1 9 9 9 0 4 2 6 6 0 *